The Silver Penny

RANDALL WRIGHT

The Silver Penny

Henry Holt and Company
New York

Henry Holt and Company, LLC
Publishers since 1866
115 West 18th Street
New York, New York 10011
www.henryholt.com

Library of Congress Cataloging-in-Publication Data
Wright, Randall.
The silver penny / Randall Wright.—1st ed.
p.   cm.
Summary: A rare silver coin and a mysterious red-haired boy seem
entangled in eleven-year-old Jacob "Deb" Corey's fate when he is laid up
with a badly broken leg on his family's farm in the mid-1800s,
just after performing a hex to cure his wanderlust.
ISBN-13: 978-0-8050-7391-1
ISBN-10: 0-8050-7391-4
[1. Luck—Fiction.   2. Talismans—Fiction.   3. Accidents—Fiction.   4. Wounds and injuries—
Fiction.   5. Supernatural—Fiction.   6. Farm life—Fiction.   7. Family life—Fiction.]   I. Title.
PZ7.W95825Si 2005   [Fic]—dc22   2004052346

First Edition—2005
Design by Patrick Collins
Printed in the United States of America on acid-free paper. ∞

1   3   5   7   9   10   8   6   4   2

For Jacob and Tyler

In memory of
Roald Emerson Peterson

The Silver Penny

Chapter One

GRANDPA HAD SAID old tales were best. He said that new tales were either too dull or too painful for the recounting. Deb didn't know about painful, but he reckoned that tedium was just a plain fact of life these days. He figured if he had to clean out Hilde's stall one more time, he'd bust. He wished he knew the hex for making all that manure disappear.

Grandpa said the German folk down in Pennsylvania knew how to do it—how to throw a powwow that would tell the future or set a broken bone or turn a whole pile of cow manure into sunshine and air. But Grandpa was old. In reality he was Pa's grandpa, and his mind wasn't what it used to be. He could barely recollect the cure for the wanderlust, let alone the more useful hexes.

There was no denying the old man was forgetful. Deb thought it funny that his great-grandpa should remember the things that happened to him away back in the War for Independence, but something as important as telling the future had plumb slipped his mind.

"Well, maybe I'll just work it out on my own," Deb told himself as he snuck down the path toward the creek.

He thought he'd start with the cure for the wanderlust. He could tell easy if it worked because he had that ailment something fearful. If his longing to pack a knapsack and light out through the new spring woods disappeared, then the cure was sure. Not that he really wanted to heal himself of the malady. He liked dreaming of all the places he'd never been. He just figured he could always get the sickness back later when it suited him. Right now it was the hexing that had his curiosity.

He'd need a toad. There were plenty along the banks of the chattering creek—he only had to poke about through the new growth of orchard grass and the damp and rotting leaves left over from last fall. He and Cousin Tam had dug for toads every spring since he could remember, but she was gone now—she and her pa had moved off to Winfield along with Deb's sister, Lydia, and her husband, Brady. Deb missed Tam. It was she who gave him his nickname, Deb. All because her baby

tongue had got tangled up around his given name—
Jacob. Some folks thought his nickname was a little funny
for a boy, but to him it sounded just fine, like it had
always been his. A gift from Cousin Tam.

But that was nothing to the point. Tam would've been
scared of the hexing.

"Aha. There you are."

A big, fat toad hunkered down in the muck beneath
the log Deb pushed aside. It blinked one lazy eye and
then the other, then flattened itself farther into the
mud. Deb reached for the toad, using a handkerchief as
a ward against the warts.

"Just hold still there," he said.

The toad seemed obliging enough, though when Deb
picked it up, its hind legs twitched in complaint. Deb
peeked over his shoulder toward the house. Ma would skin
him if she knew what he was up to. She didn't hold with
Grandpa's talk of magic or charms—not in her Christian
house. She wouldn't even let Grandpa hide a shoe up the
chimney to keep the bad luck from slipping in.

So despite Ma's Good Book warnings wrangling
about in the back of his head, Deb crept into the orchard
toward the burning place with the toad squelched up in
his hand. His twelfth birthday would be next week. He
might as well deserve some of the birthday licks Pa was
going to give him.

With another look over his shoulder, he snuck out into the sun-drenched clearing. A pile of ashes marked the place where this year's prunings had already been burned. Ma said they should save the twigs and branches for kindling in the fireplace, but Grandpa was hard-headed about that. She could do what she liked with the house, he said, but the orchard was his. He insisted that the virtue of the cuttings, pruned under the last full moon of winter, be returned to the soil.

The bang of a closing door echoed through the morning air. At any moment Ma would discover Deb wasn't in the barn cleaning Hilde's stall. He hadn't much time. With his heel he dug a circle in the dirt, near two feet across. He placed the toad in the center and recited the words Grandpa had taught him.

"Feet a-turning—"

The toad hopped out of the circle.

"Dang it, get back here."

He scooped up the toad and set it in its place.

"Feet a-turning, heart a-churning—"

The toad jumped off toward the apple trees. Hunched over, Deb chased after it, snatching at tufts of grass and empty air.

"C'mon, you . . . gotcha!"

The toad squirmed out of his grip and leapt toward freedom, but Deb snagged it by the leg.

"Now, you stay put."

The toad blinked its eyes. It opened and closed its mouth. Deb blurted out the words as fast as he could remember them:

> *FEET A-TURNING,*
> *HEART A-CHURNING,*
> *YEARNINGS OF A BODY FREE.*
> *HEARTH A-WARMING,*
> *HOMEWARD CALLING*
> *BACK TO DOMESTICITY.*

The toad shifted about to face the morning sun. It squinched its eyes closed in the warmth and remained in the circle.

"It works," Deb cried. "The hex works!"

To test his own feelings, he gazed down the long rows of apple trees and opened his heart to the full lure of springtime. White blossoms fluttered in the air, spinning and twirling like a sweet-smelling snowfall. Sunlight dappled the earth beneath the branches, turning the spurge and orchard grass a golden green. Deb looked up into the deep blue of the sky. A breeze touched his cheek. He felt an itching to head out, striding longlegged through the trees and over the hills to see all the wild places Grandpa had told him about.

"Drat!"

The hex hadn't worked at all. The whole of outdoors was conspiring against him.

Deb kicked at the toad and sent it hopping away toward the creek. Maybe Grandpa had remembered the spell wrong.

"Young man! Why aren't you about your chores?"

Deb gulped. Ma stood beneath an apple tree, wiping her hands on her apron. He hoped she hadn't heard the hex. She wouldn't wait for his birthday to use the willow switch. He shuffled his feet about in the dirt to hide the circle.

"You get back to the barn," she said. "Your pa would wear you out if he found you here, 'stead of doing your chores."

Deb breathed in relief. "Yes'm."

"Now, get busy."

"Yes'm."

"And when you've finished in the barn, your pa will need you out in the field. You know he's plowing today and could use your help. Now, get."

"Yes'm."

Deb followed Ma out of the orchard, lagging behind as much as he dared. As she stalked off toward the house, Deb trudged to the barn. His yearning to pack a knapsack burned stronger than ever.

"Dull," he muttered. "Just plain dull."

He led Hilde out of her stall and tied her to a post. She would be calving soon and so was tended here in the barn instead of out in the meadow with the rest of the cattle. It would be her first birth, so Pa wanted to keep a close watch on her.

Deb pitched the straw and manure into a wheelbarrow. He wished Tam were there. At least she would understand his feelings—even if he were tempted to toss a pitchfork of dirty straw in her hair. He grinned at the thought.

Once the stall was cleaned and new straw spread about, Deb paused to rest. He was in no hurry to get out to the field to help Pa with the plowing, to stand ready in case Pa had something for him to fetch or to pull another rock from beneath the plow's blade.

He shuffled over to Betsy's stall, leaving Hilde to chew her cud. "You're lucky," he said, stroking the old mare's neck. "At least you don't have to pull the plow no more."

And then he had an idea. "You wanna go for a ride?"

He figured he might as well earn the rest of those birthday licks.

Chapter Two

CLEAR OVER at the farm in Winfield, Tam peeked into the root cellar. Her hand clutched fast the rickety door, like she couldn't decide whether to go in or just leave it be. It wasn't that she was scared of spiders or other creepy things. It was only that she didn't trust the dark, especially after waking up this morning to such a terrible premonition. She couldn't remember if it had been a dream or a conscious thought that had left her feeling twitchy inside, but she knew it had something to do with Cousin Deb and trouble.

Standing in the doorway, she wished she had a lantern. A body could never be sure what was waiting inside all that blackness. Squirming bugs were one thing, but folk from the unseen world were altogether another. Though a lantern would've helped, Pa wouldn't allow her to use one in the daytime. He said it was a waste of oil, and with their new farm mortgaged up to Mr. Simons, they didn't dare to spare a drop. So Tam had to be quick to beat whatever might be lurking there.

She was after turnips.

The cool, damp air of the cellar brushed her face like spiderwebs. It smelled of moldering earth, winter-old taters, wet burlap, and darkness. The gunnysack full of turnips was set along the far wall. Carrots were close, right inside the door, but those weren't what Pa wanted. She inched forward, letting her eyes grow accustomed to the dim interior before she had to leave the sunlight at her back. Her heart rattled up against her insides, making her want to skinny back out into the day.

Tam shook her hands at her sides. "Just hurry," she whispered. And so she did, but in her hurry she stumbled over a lump of something on the floor. She fell head-first into a bag of taters—she could tell by their sour smell.

She scrambled forward, tore open a sack, and, quick as a squirrel, scurried out into daylight with four turnips clutched to her chest. But her heart continued its hammering. It seemed the darkness had chased out into the yard with her. She hurried to sit on the milking stool beneath the chestnut tree to calm herself but missed and landed plop on the ground with her skirt flying up about her. She nearly lost the turnips.

"Drat!"

The scared feeling wouldn't leave. It was just like the premonition of this morning—a gloom in the bright light of day. It was the same feeling she had had when Ma took ill and never got any better. And no matter how much Tam shook her head and stomped her feet, the feeling wouldn't leave her be.

"Deb," she whispered. And then she fell to sobbing into the turnips for no reason she could tell.

Chapter Three

*D*EB COULDN'T REMEMBER whether Grandpa had said a hawk sitting on a fence was good luck or bad. Grandpa knew all the portents—horseshoes, iron nails bent south, hooting owls—but as Deb rode Betsy out from the barn he couldn't remember what Grandpa had said about hawks.

Deb spied the fierce-looking bird perched on the fence post clear up across the yard, beneath the twin oak trees. It looked so strong and wild, he decided it must be good luck. Still, he steered Betsy away from the house and Ma, just to be sure.

"C'mon." Deb clicked his tongue. "Move them old legs."

Though Betsy no longer had to pull the plow, she was

still plenty game. Deb raced her along the fence, his knees squeezed tight to keep from bouncing off her bare back. The hawk leapt into the sky with a sweeping flap of wings. Betsy's hooves dug up muddy clods of earth that rained back to the ground behind them.

"Yeehaw!" Deb cried.

They swept around the yard and galloped toward the orchard. The wind in his hair and the whipping of Betsy's mane in his face felt so grand, he didn't care whether Ma saw him now or not. He turned the mare back toward the field and headed straight for the fence.

"Let's see if you're still a jumper," he said.

Betsy's breath came in snorts as she pounded up the hillside. Deb could feel her gathering for the leap. But then she slipped, her front legs splaying before her. She slid sideways and crashed through the fence. Deb flew through the air. He almost laughed at the thrill of it, but when he hit the ground, a jolting blow sent a shock of pain through his body.

In a daze, he tried to move, but the hurt was more than he could bear. All he could do was lie there and stare at the sky. The hawk soared high overhead, its out-stretched wings silhouetted against the deep blue of spring.

Must be bad *luck*, Deb thought, and then his mind fluttered away with the hawk.

Chapter Four

"WHAT ARE ALL them tears about, then?"

Startled, Tam wiped her nose with the back of her hand. "What? Who's there?" She looked about the yard but could see no one—not up to the house, not under the old, broken-down wagon left behind by the Mechams, not back by the root cellar.

"Where are you?" she said.

"Crying over turnips, eh?"

She looked up into a pair of bright eyes that peered at her from within the branches of the chestnut tree. She jumped to her feet in alarm, scattering the turnips all about.

"Who are you?" she asked. "What're you doing up there?"

A strange boy sat on a limb amongst the new-budded leaves, kicking his bare feet. "Just looking for something," he said.

Tam backed away. "Up in our tree?"

The boy shrugged. "You can see a long ways from here." He swung down from the branch to hang by one arm. "'Sides, a chestnut tree is good luck. Especially with me in it." He dropped to the ground.

He was dressed in just a pair of raggedy overalls, with only a single strap to hold them up. A pile of red hair tumbled down on his forehead.

"You better clean yourself up," he said. His voice had a strange lilt to it. Almost like he was singing. "Your pa'll know you been crying for something you can do naught about."

Tam wiped her face on her sleeve. "What do you mean?"

"I mean your face is dirty—all messed up with crying."

"It's not."

"You know best." He shielded his eyes with both hands and stared at the sun. "Well, I guess I oughta be going now. Mayhaps I was mistaken. What I'm looking for can't be here." He spun about and trotted off toward the road.

"Wait . . ."

With a turn of his head, he called back, "Don't worry, he ain't dead yet. But you best take care of him."

Chapter Five

For a time Deb dreamed he was a toad. Caught up by his hind leg, he twitched and squirmed to free himself from some monster's grip. But he was caught good. The more he wriggled about, the more crooked his leg turned, until he wondered how he would ever walk again. Finally, he managed to pull himself half awake, but the burning fever seemed reluctant to release him completely. In this half-dream, he found himself lying in the yard before the empty house. A ragged old man scratched a hex-circle about him in the dirt. "This boy is mine," the man said. The sound shivered Deb's insides.

"Heart a-churning," the old man continued, "soul a-burning, longings that will never be. . . ."

In the distance Deb spied a glimmer. It appeared out

of nowhere, giving him something to cling to—something to pull him away from the old man's hex. He caught hold of the glimmer and held on.

But the wizened old voice hissed, "You'll not escape so easy."

Deb squeezed tight the silver light.

Chapter Six

THE MORNING Deb's sister, Lydia, received the letter from her ma, Tam was busy rattling through her household chores, having forgotten all about premonitions and unseen things in the dark. She had just begun sweeping off the hearth when Lydia and Pa came in.

"Deb's been hurt," Pa said. "Real bad. Throwed from a horse three days ago. Mr. Greenfield just brought along a note from Deb's ma."

"Deb's hurt?" And then Tam remembered. The dark root cellar. Turnips. And a strange boy.

Her stomach squeezed tight, balling up her insides. "How bad?"

Lydia wore a troubled look on her face. "We must pray for him."

Pa wiped his face with his handkerchief. "I reckon we can do more than pray. We'll leave first thing in the morning. Lydia, you and Brady can take the buggy. It'll be easier on the baby. Tam, you and me'll go in the buckboard."

Tam nodded despite the tears that trickled down her cheeks. Pa and Brady wouldn't be so willing to leave the spring planting unless there was good reason. Unless Deb was beyond hurt and near to dying.

"I'll take care of him," she said.

Lydia put an arm around her shoulder. "We all will."

Chapter Seven

*T*HOUGH *D*EB *STILL* trailed bits of darkness along behind him, it was the silver light that pulled him back. Slowly his vision blurred into focus. A patch of brightness fluttered against the whitewashed ceiling overhead. Grateful to escape from what seemed like more than a dream, he tried to stretch out, but a stabbing pain shot up his leg, making his eyes go dim again. With a groan, he sank back into the feather mattress. The little patch of light slid down the wall and disappeared.

"Ma?" he called. "Ma, where are you?"

He heard a clattering on the wooden stairs.

"Ma-a-a!"

"I'm here, I'm here." She rushed into the loft, pushing

at her hair with the back of a hand. "Thank goodness! You're awake. I've been so worried."

Deb searched about, looking for the man who had threatened to trap him in his hex. Only sunlight whispered in the corners.

"Ma," he said, "what's happened? Why am I in bed?"

She felt his forehead. "We thought you were going to leave us."

"Leave you? How could I do that?"

"We prayed you wouldn't."

He struggled to sit up, but Ma gently pushed him back down.

"You stay put," she said.

"But I feel fine."

The lie was no match for Ma. "No, you don't. Now just lay quiet. I'll be right back." She hurried down the stairs.

Again, Deb tried to squirm himself to a sitting position, but the effort made him light-headed. He lay back and parceled out his breath. He didn't want to disturb the spinning of the bed.

"I still want to get up."

He flexed the toes on his right foot, hoping to ease the itch of his leg, but even that movement made him dizzy with pain.

"Ma," he called to the ceiling, "I need some water."

He lifted the covers and peeked down at his leg. It was bound from ankle to thigh in white bandages that were tied tight around a wood splint. He tried to recall what had happened. And then he remembered Betsy.

"Ma-a-a—"

But she was already at the top of the stairs with a cup in one hand and bowl of something in the other. Deb took the cup and drank greedily, dribbling water down his chin.

"Not so fast," Ma said. "You've been three days with no more than a few spoonfuls."

He pulled the cup away. "Three days?"

Ma nodded. She helped him to a sitting position with the pillow behind his back and then handed him the bowl. "A little broth will get your strength up."

"What happened to Betsy?"

She put a hand to his forehead. "First, how do you *really* feel?"

"Like a fence post."

"Oh? A fence post?"

"Like I've been stuck here forever."

"Just be glad you're still with us. Pa's gone to tell Doc Williams that you've come around. The doc didn't think there was much hope."

"But what about Betsy?"

"Never you mind. You just—" She stopped with a

puzzled look on her face. "What in tarnation?" She reached across the bed and picked up a small silver object. Its reflection flashed on the ceiling.

"Let me see," Deb said.

"It must be Grandpa's. One of his luck pieces. That old fool."

"Can I see it?"

She held the object up between two fingers. It was a silver penny, shiny bright, almost like new, except for the figure of an old, dead king on its face. It was a Tory coin from before the War for Independence.

Its sparkling glitter reminded Deb of something, but he couldn't quite remember what. "Maybe he lost it. By accident."

Ma slid the penny into her apron pocket. "I reckon he put it here a' purpose. One of his charms to try and get you well." She shook her head. "What you really need is rest."

"But when can I get up?"

"When your strength's returned," she said.

"Maybe tomorrow?"

She looked at the ceiling and sighed. "Eat your soup."

That afternoon, Ma returned to the loft with another bowl of broth. She was followed by Doc Williams and Pa, whose face was dark with sweat and dirt from the field. Grandpa came, too, but he hung back at the top of the stairs.

"Well, son," the doc said, "let's have a look."

Ma pulled down the covers. Deb shivered when she lifted up his nightshirt. His foot was all swelled up and bruised to a greenish yellow.

"Lie back," the doc commanded. He began to unwrap the bandage. In a kinder voice he added, "Your ma tells me you want to get out of bed."

Deb stared at the ceiling and nodded with the pain. "Yes, sir."

"Well, we'll see. I reckon it's a miracle you're here at all." Then Doc Williams clucked his tongue.

Deb lifted himself up to look, but Pa gently pushed him back down.

"What's happened to my leg?" Deb cried. "Why's it all tore up?"

"Your leg's broke," Pa said. "The bone busted through the skin, but don't you fret, the doc pulled it all back together. You'll be fine now."

"Might as well tell you," Doc Williams said, "walking is going to be a mite difficult."

"Till when?" Ma asked.

"Look how the leg is twisted there, Mrs. Corey. I set it best I could. Don't know what else I could do."

"Will it stop hurting?" Deb asked.

"Yes, son. It'll heal."

Deb cried out as Doc Williams lifted the injured leg.

"Hush," Ma said. She took his hand. "He's got to wrap it again."

After the bandaging, the doc gave Deb a small cup to drink. "It'll ease the pain and help you to rest."

When they finally left Deb alone, he was all tuckered out. Grandpa was the last to go. He stood at the top of the stairs and smiled from beneath his white mustache.

"Grandpa, stay," Deb pleaded, seeking comfort from the doctor's words.

"Your ma wants me to leave you to your rest," the old man said. "But maybe I can sneak up a little later with a story or two."

"Grandpa, that hex you told me about must have worked."

"What hex?"

"The cure for wanderlust. The one with the toad. It must have worked. Look at me. I'll not be wandering anywhere ever again!"

Grandpa only shook his head.

It was dark outside by the time Grandpa found his way back to Deb's room. Deb had just finished the dinner Ma brought up, and now he listened to Grandpa's creak-

SEE ON
PUBLIC LIBRARY

ing voice, echoed by the chirp of crickets through the open window. Deb caught a whiff of blossoms hanging on the breeze.

"Froze 'em clean off," Grandpa said, meaning his toes. "Yes, sir. That winter it was cold at Valley Forge. Why, I knew a feller standing sentry duty one night, stood so long in one place that when he went to breakfast muster, he left a foot behind, froze to the ground. Bad luck for whoever found it next spring."

Deb near choked on his laugh. Then the picture of the crippled soldier flashed into his mind, and he frowned. "Poor man."

"Er, yep. Poor man." Grandpa frowned, too, and shook his head. "But that was a long time ago." There was no hiding the glister in the old man's eyes.

"You mean to say you lost *all* your toes?" Deb asked.

"Uh-huh." Grandpa stamped his feet. "But they got better. And now it's getting late. So get to sleep. And don't dream nothing but pleasant."

"I'll try."

Grandpa gave Deb a bristly kiss on the forehead, then shuffled to the stairs and down, forgetting to blow out the light that reflected yellow through its hurricane globe.

After a bit Ma came grumbling into the room. "Don't I have enough to do?"

She bent to the lamp and puffed out its flame. Then she closed the window by Deb's bed, shutting out the sound of the crickets.

"Good night, Ma," Deb whispered.

She turned in the darkness. "Good night, darling."

He was surprised at the sudden softness in her voice.

"You sleep well." She sat on the edge of his bed.

"Ma?"

"Yes, son?"

"Is Betsy dead?"

Deb could just see her nod in the darkness.

"Was her leg broke, too?" he asked.

"Yes."

"Too muddy for jumping."

"Yes, it was. And that fence too high, and poor Betsy too old." She wiped her face with a hand. "And spring too early to be nearly killed before the planting's even done."

Deb tried to clear the lump out of his throat. "Ma, what'd the doc mean—what he said about me walking?"

He couldn't even hear her breathing, like she had sucked in her last breath and wouldn't let it out again.

"Ma?"

"You know what he said." Her voice went tight and

matter-of-fact again. "Your leg's like to cripple up a bit. Now I've got things to do. I'll see you in the morning."

"Ma, what'd you do with that penny?"

"I gave it back to Grandpa. Told him to keep his charms out of my house. You get some sleep, now. You still need rest. We've got to get your leg mended before harvest."

"Yes, Ma."

Despite Ma and Grandpa's good wishes, Deb didn't have much luck at all sleeping that night. He was tormented again by the feeling of being held like a toad, squirming against a grip that wouldn't let go. Whispers came out of the darkness, flitting about the room with a rustle of wings. *Heart a-churning, soul a-burning. . . .* He struggled to shut out the sound with his pillow tugged up against his ears. Then sometime long past midnight, an unexpected, pleasant drowse crept out of the darkness to settle in his heart and mind, rescuing him from the torment. Finally he dropped off and slept a far sight better than he had in days—still and hardly moving. Deep and quiet. His dreams were less jumbled about and worried than they had been.

When he awoke to the new day, he felt nearly rested. He hitched himself up to sitting and breathed deep, letting his chest stretch against his nightshirt. He watched the pattern of blue morning light flutter across his bed. And then he spied it, just at his feet, lying on the quilt: the silver penny with the figure of some old king turned to face the window.

Chapter Eight

A WARM COMFORT eased itself up the length of the bed, like it seeped out of the coin itself. Still drowsy with sleep, Deb nudged at the penny with his good foot. It rose and fell like a leaf caught up in a current. He wiggled his toes, and the penny shimmered in the ripples he made.

"Now, where'd you come from?" he asked.

The silver figure continued its mute gaze out the window.

"Did Grandpa bring you up here? Or are you just about your own business?"

He wiggled his toes at it once more. The coin flashed. "I wish I could reach you," he whispered.

"Who you talking to up there?" called a voice from the stairs. It was Grandpa.

"Morning," Deb said.

"Morning, boy." Grandpa trudged into the loft. "You got pixies up here?"

"Naw. Just me."

"Well, good morning then, *just you*. You're looking a sight better. Not as peaked as you was. Wanna wrassle?"

"I could best you, Grandpa."

"Like to make a little wager on that?"

"All I've got is a penny."

"Now where'd *you* get a penny?"

"I reckon you left it here again."

"What?"

"Look there on the bed."

"Why, I—" Grandpa shoved a hand into his pocket. "I could have sworn. . . ." He pulled the hand out empty. With a frown, he rummaged about in his other pocket.

"You must have dropped it," Deb said.

Grandpa picked up the coin. His eyebrows bristled. "I could have sworn I left it. . . ." He turned his eyes back toward the stairs. "Your ma would skin me if—"

"It's old, isn't it?" Deb asked.

Grandpa lowered himself into the rocking chair that Ma had kept at the head of the bed. "Old? Yep. Older 'n me, even. This here is George the Second. Was his grand-boy that caused us so much trouble away back yonder in the war."

"Where'd you get it?"

"Hmph. Now, that's a story."

Deb leaned forward and waited for Grandpa to continue, but the old man seemed to have wandered off in his own thoughts. Deb could hear his wheezing, still heavy from climbing the stairs.

Finally Grandpa shook his head. "Stories are for bedtime. But seeing how this thing wants to stay here with you, why don't you just keep it till then?" He creaked out of the chair, straightening his aging joints the best he could. "But don't tell your ma." He handed Deb the coin.

Deb turned the penny over and settled it on the flat of his palm. "Grandpa, there's writing on it." He followed the lettering around the outer edge of the coin. Crude characters had been scratched over the monarch's name.

"*D.T.O.M.* What's that mean?"

Grandpa chuckled. "*Don't Tread on Me*, it says."

Deb thought for a moment and then laughed, too. That old Colonial battle motto was a funny joke to play on the British monarch. "Who put it there?"

"Hmph. Stories are for—"

"I know. Bedtime."

"Yup. And you need to stay rested today. Lydia's coming. And Brady and your Uncle Andy. Young Jenks from Winfield stopped by on his way through to Almond Township just this morning. Brought a note from your sister."

"Uncle Andy? And Tam, too?"

"You don't figure they'd leave your cousin home alone, do you?"

"They're coming for my birthday?"

Grandpa shook his head. "They're coming 'cause you was almost killed."

"Grandpa, do you reckon she's changed?" Over the months his cousin's image had begun to blur in his mind. Though he could still recollect bits of her face and features, he couldn't quite piece them all together.

"It's been a long while, ain't it?" Grandpa said.

"Almost a year."

"Well, I expect she's changed some. But I've a feeling it won't matter. You two was always a pair. Like them salt and pepper shakers your ma never uses. I thought the two of you would just crumple to dust being broke apart like you was. Why, I'll wager when old Betsy busted through that fence and sent you a-flying, Tam hollered from the scare of it, clear off in Winfield."

"Well, I hope she doesn't go making a fuss over me."

Grandpa's face wrinkled up around his eyes and squeezed out a sparkle. "Well, you know the women-folk."

Deb turned quiet. For a while Grandpa's wheezing was the only sound.

Then Deb broke the silence. "Tam's out on the early morning road in the sun and springtime, and I can't do nothing but lie here like a sack."

"Now, boy."

"It's true! I can't even get up to throw scratch to the chickens." With the thought of his cousin's cheerful energy, the full import of the doctor's words the day before settled hard on Deb. The pleasant feeling he had on waking fled clean away. He felt the monster pulling at him all over again.

"I might just as well be dead," he said. He wriggled down into the bed as far as he was able.

"Son . . ."

But Deb had no more words for Grandpa.

Chapter Nine

P<small>A,</small>" T<small>AM CALLED</small> from her place in the back of the wagon. "When we gonna be there?"

The last milepost seemed ages ago and the countryside was as unchanged as when they first set out in the early morning light.

"In time for supper," Pa answered. He twisted in his seat to glance back at her. "At least afore dark. Now quit your fretting."

"Yes, Pa."

But it was barely getting on to noon with a whole afternoon of worry yet before them. Tam sighed out her impatience and lay back against the blankets and bedding. The wool of them scratched her neck. A baby's cry drifted from the buggy up ahead. Conner was fussing to be fed.

Deb had yet to see his spanking-new nephew. Tam wondered if he ever would. The letter from Aunt Mary said he was nigh on to dying, lying near lifeless in a fever. Tam wished the horses would move faster.

She gazed at the blue of the sky—a spring blue, high and light and clear. A swirl of chattering birds gusted away over the wagon, carrying their gossip to settle in a tree bright with new leaves and blossoms. As she listened to their raucous chirping, her stomach took to a nervous fluttering itself, like she had swallowed a whole flock of birds. What if Deb was already dead? She tried not to think about it.

She and Deb had always been close. Grandpa had once accused them of having their insides all tangled together. When Deb was whipped for busting up the buttermilk crock, it was Tam that cried.

A smile bunched up her cheeks. She remembered one bitter-cold morning a few winters back, when Deb had broken the ice on the creek to draw water and then fallen in just to make her laugh. His teeth chattered all the way back home. It was a wonder he hadn't caught his death. Her smile turned soft. When Ma passed on that same winter, it was Deb who had wrapped his arms about his younger cousin to squeeze some warmth back into her heart. But that was ages ago, and by now he might even have forgotten that she had been the one to give him his nickname.

"Pa, you think Jacob'll remember me?"

Pa spat his chaw of tobacco out into the road. "*Jacob*, eh? Well, maybe if you two'd written more."

"Deb's not much of a writer."

"I know, hon. Always something else to do. He's such a busy boy. I figure that's what got him into trouble so much. And this time—"

Tam sat up straight. "Look, Pa," she cried.

"I see."

Up ahead the buggy had rolled to a stop. Tam clambered into the seat beside her pa. "What is it?"

"Looks like somebody's hurt. Whoa, Black, whoa, Chinny." He pulled the horses up and leapt from the buckboard. Tam followed close behind. Lydia's husband, Brady, was already squatting in the dust. A boy lay stretched on his back at the side of the road.

Brady shook him. "He's knocked out cold," he said.

"Or sleeping," Pa said. "He don't seem to be hurt."

Tam peeked into the boy's face. His eyes flickered behind closed lids, and his breathing came deep and regular.

"Why, I've seen him before! He was at the farm a few days ago. 'Member I told you? Up in the chestnut tree. Looking for something, he said."

The boy's calm was interrupted by a ragged snore. He rolled to his side, snorted again, and stretched a bare arm straight up to the sky. With eyes blinking from under a thatch of dusty, red hair, he sat himself up and looked around.

"Hey, you!" Brady yelled as if the boy might be deaf. "Are you all right?"

The boy stared at him and ran a tongue over dry lips.

"Tam, fetch me some water," Brady said. "From behind the seat. There's a jug."

Tam obeyed, but in her hurry the skirt of her dress caught up on the long-step, and she was yanked back into the road, falling hard on her bottom.

"Ow!"

"Be careful," Lydia said. "You all right?"

With the dust still settling, Tam rubbed her backside. "I'm fine—"

A loud guffaw exploded from someone behind her. She looked around. The ragged boy was doubled over, giggling and snorting.

"I reckon he's all right, too," Brady said.

Pa helped Tam to her feet. "Have you hurt yourself?"

She dusted herself off. "That wasn't funny."

The boy stopped laughing, though his mouth was still spread in a wide grin. "Naw, not for you." He sprang to his feet. "But it's a grand day, ain't it?" He stood up on his toes and looked all about. "Grand!"

"Yep, it's a fine 'un," Pa said. "Now, what are you doing here in the middle of nowhere? Where's your folks?"

The boy stuck out his hand. "Spare a penny?"

"I'm sorry," Pa said, "but we have none."

"I've packed a lunch," Lydia said. "We can spare a bit of that."

The boy gave her a strange, sad look, like he was remembering something he had long forgotten. "And you with a baby. Thank'ee." But then his face brightened again. "I best be on my way." He spun about and lit off up the hillside.

"Now where's he going to?" Lydia said.

Before anyone could answer, the boy had disappeared into the woods.

Pa looked befuddled. "I reckon he was just napping."

"Well, I don't figure he's from around here," Brady said. "He sure had a strange way of talking."

Tam had already settled on her opinion of the boy. "He's an idiot," she muttered, rubbing her bruised backside.

"Well, he's run off to someplace," Pa said. "And in a mighty big hurry."

"And we better get on ourselves." Lydia looked up at the noon sky. "Or we shan't be getting to Mamma's before dark."

As Pa shook the reins to get the horses moving again, Tam peeked back into the woods where the impudent boy had disappeared. And there she spied him, following along from tree to tree, watching from beneath the branches. Then she lost him in the shadows, and though she kept an eye out, she didn't see him again through the whole rest of the afternoon.

The sun was just touching on the horizon, burning it bright with orange and gold, when they finally arrived at Aunt Mary's and Uncle Arley's. The house itself stood in long shadows of poplar trees, back away from the road. Tam half expected to see her cousin jump down from the porch and race them to the gate, but then she remembered. The fear returned to flutter through her stomach. "Please be there," she whispered.

As soon as the wagon rolled to a stop in front of the house, Aunt Mary came out to the porch, followed by Uncle Arley and Grandpa.

"Well," said Pa from his seat, "how is he?"

Tam held her breath, looking for a hint in their faces.

"Oh, that boy," Aunt Mary said with a sigh. "He wasn't made to stay in bed."

Tam paused at the bottom of the stairs that led up to the loft. With her hand on the wall, she shook off the premonition that had returned the moment she stepped inside the house, the feeling that something was wrong. It wasn't the house, nor the day, but something clutched at her with a sharp, wriggling claw. She glanced upward. Aunt Mary had said everything was fine, there was nothing to worry about now. Deb was going to be all right.

"Go on," Grandpa said from behind. "He could use a little cheering. You might just as well be the first, while everyone else is trying to bring their visit into the house."

At Grandpa's urging, Tam hurried up the stairs, but she stopped short at the top, shocked by the appearance of her cousin. He was nothing like she remembered. His bright, cheerful face seemed sallow and sunken, his body small and frail. It was like a gauzy shadow had been draped over his features.

"Hullo," she said, dropping her gaze to the floor.

"Hullo."

"How are you feeling?" she asked.

"Fine."

Even his voice sounded flat and dull. Not like she remembered at all. She brought herself to look at his face again. He was staring out the window now. She moved to the foot of the bed.

"I'm sure glad that wagon ride is over." She tried to laugh. "My backside is plumb past feeling from the sitting." She was too embarrassed to mention her fall.

"When did you leave?" Deb asked, his gaze still fixed outside.

"After the milking. Just after sunup. Though Pa did let me walk a bit."

"He let you walk?"

"Well, it was better than sitting the whole way. How are you feeling?"

"You already asked me that."

"Oh. . . . Does it hurt?" She felt at a loss for anything else to say.

"Course it hurts, what do you figure? Like it's a walk on the road?"

"I . . . I'm sorry. I just—"

A gravelly voice interrupted her from the top of the stairs. "It's good to see you two together again."

Tam ran into Grandpa's arms, trying to hold back the tears.

"Grandpa, he *is* changed," she whispered.

"Now, now. He'll be fine. He's still the same old Deb."

"No he isn't. Can't you see it? He's changed." She shivered again at the premonition. "Something's got hold of him."

The old man gave her a squeeze. "Well, Tam, you'll just have to stay with us for a while and help him recollect who he is."

Chapter Ten

*D*EB WAS GRATEFUL Grandpa's story wasn't just another attempt to cheer him up. And he was relieved Tam mostly kept quiet through the telling. Her chattering had turned bothersome, though Deb felt guilty about feeling that way. Right now she lay at the foot of the bed, stretched across the quilt in her nightgown, trying to muffle her yawns in folded arms. Grandpa sat hunched over in the rocking chair, his arms braced against his knees, his story finished—ended with a deep sigh and then silence.

"Well," he said at last, "you've found me out."

"What d'you mean?" Deb asked.

"I never was at Valley Forge. I still have all my toes."

He half smiled. "It's like I told you—true stories can be a sight more painful."

Moonlight glimmered through the bedside window. Grandpa's age seemed more marked in that silvery gloom—his white hair glistened, the furrows and crannies of his face stood out in the shadows.

Deb held the penny up in the moonlight, trying to see it just as Grandpa had on that fearsome night so long ago. "But how could you have borne it all?" He weighed the tragic story against his own desperate feelings.

Grandpa shook his head. "What else was there to do?"

"Nothing, I expect. But do you think it's magic?"

Grandpa shrugged. "Just good luck, I reckon." He glanced toward the foot of the bed. "For some, at least." Tam's breathing came low and regular. As if in sympathy to her exhaustion, Grandpa yawned wide himself and stretched back in his chair.

"Poor Tam," he said at the tail end of his yawn. "She's mighty tired. Nothing harder on a body than sitting all day in a wagon." He stood, leaving the chair to creak and sway from his motion.

"Can I keep it?" Deb asked.

With a grunt, Grandpa lifted Tam in his arms. "I don't figure it's mine to give."

"Why not?"

"Hush, now. You don't want to wake her. 'Sides, it was only loaned to me."

"But that was ages ago."

"Yep. Ages ago." He paused for a moment. "I reckon you're right. I don't suppose anyone could be coming for it now. And I expect I don't need the luck no more. Maybe we can make it my birthday present to you?"

Deb opened his hand to peer at the coin. "I'll take good care of it."

With Tam cradled in his arms, Grandpa shuffled across the floor. He stopped at the top of the stairs and puffed out his breath. Then he hobbled down into the darkness below. After a moment Deb could hear Ma's scolding—a half whisper gauged to show her anger without disturbing anybody already asleep. Deb wondered why she was so distrustful of Grandpa. Was it his age? He fell to calculating. Grandpa would have been just fourteen at the time of his story about the penny. Only two years older than Deb.

"Poor Grandpa."

Deb looked out the window. Though the moon had risen beyond his view, it shone so bright he could almost feel its light upon his face.

Must be nearly full, he thought.

Then he yawned, too. He hadn't slept at all that day, and now that night was here, he felt a drowsiness tugging at his eyelids. With the silver penny still clutched in his hand, he hunkered down between the covers.

Lying alone there in the dark, the portent behind the doctor's words returned to nag at him, so he hung on tight to the coin, sure now that its luck would protect him from the voice of his illness. A warmth stole up his arm, bringing with it the memory of Grandpa's tale. The old man's words had been so earnest Deb didn't doubt them, not this time. He fell to pondering what he would have done in such a fix.

Young Alvin Corey had itched to be a part of the fight for independence. He itched to fight alongside the heroes of the Continental army. When word arrived that a Tory force was set to invade their peaceful Pennsylvania valley, he was all set to go. But his pa and two older brothers, Rufus and Benjamin, told him no. They would be the ones to enlist in the volunteer militia at Forty Fort. Alvin would be left behind to look after his ma and the three little ones.

Alvin was having none of that. On the morning of the muster, he snuck one of his pa's vests, smudged his chin with dust-whiskers, shoved a scrap of cloth in his cheek as a wad of chewing tobacco, and snuck off to the fort. With his squirrel gun stowed over his shoulder like a regular musket, he hung about the fringes of the crowd, trying to look like he belonged.

By midmorning, however, the heat of the sun and the slobber from the wad had sent the dust-whiskers streaking down his chin. He spat out the "chaw" and inched into the stockade's shadows while all those around him talked and joked about the coming skirmish. He clenched his hands tight behind his back, attempting a natural pose, but still the time crept along.

When at last the order was given to march, he hitched his squirrel gun up on his shoulder and fell into step with the rearmost of the ragtag column. He knew his pa and two brothers would be away up ahead in the rising dust storm of their procession, so he reckoned he was safe from discovery. A fidgety pride swelled within him at finding himself in step with both the Colonial regulars and the volunteer militia.

"Good day, Alvin Corey."

Startled, he looked up to see a familiar profile. It was Mr. Turley, a Connecticut man.

"Good day," Alvin answered, quick-shuffling to put himself back into step. His heart had dropped clean down into his belly at Mr. Turley's greeting. After all his caution, was he going to be called out and sent back to his ma?

"Square them shoulders up if you want to be a soldier."

Alvin obeyed, sticking out his chest.

"No, not like a peacock, boy. Straight up, not puffed out."

Alvin let out the breath he had sucked in.

"And keep your eyes up front. That's better. Does your pa know you're with us?"

"My pa?"

"Your pa. Does he— Well, never mind. I reckon we need every gun we can get."

Alvin stole a quick glance at the man. Mr. Turley smiled—a slight upturn of his lips that Alvin took for approval. He marched on in relief, stepping back into the rhythm of the troop.

After a bit Mr. Turley cleared his throat. "For luck," he said, holding out a bit of something in his hand.

"What's that?"

"My luck piece. Take it."

"But—"

"It's all right. You can give it back later. You just might need it today."

Alvin tucked the small silver object into his vest pocket. "Yes, sir." He set his eyes forward again. "I'll keep it safe."

"Quiet now, boy." Mr. Turley lowered his voice to a whisper. "Here it begins to get serious."

Alvin shut his mouth tight in obedience.

Except for the tramping feet and the jangling of the soldiers' gear, the hike continued in silence through the warm noon. A film of dust caked Alvin's sweaty brow. He ducked his head and tried to rub the grime off onto his shirtsleeve. He hoped it would be cooler once they reached the trees. He had a hankering to ask Mr. Turley how far there was yet to the enemy encampment, but he didn't care to sound a nuisance. So he kept his peace and wondered whether the object of their march might not be just around the next bend.

It wasn't until late afternoon that they finally came to a halt. They had slogged steadily along the Susquehanna River, skirting the swamps and at last entering a sunny meadow. The red coats of the British army stood out against the summer green.

Alvin's jaw near dropped off his head at their numbers. From where he stood he could make out the glint of bayonets that formed a bristling line five ranks deep, stretched full along the far side of the meadow. Gripping his own gun, he glanced at a grim-faced Mr. Turley.

"Keep my luck piece close," the man said.

"Yes, sir."

The Colonial column counted off, their shouts echoing from the trees across the way, but Alvin could barely stammer out his "one." The soldiers formed two lines facing the redcoats, one rank before the other. With his heart almost banging out of his chest, Alvin stood in the front line and fidgeted with his load and primer.

But it was a useless action. Through all that fight, Alvin never once pulled the trigger of his musket. Though the order to fire was barked down the column, by the time he had a redcoat target fixed in his sights, his line had already sent its first volley toward the enemy and begun to reload. The alternate rank stepped forward through the line and discharged its barrage, squirting plumes of smoke across the field. Alvin struggled to keep up as the divided company by turns advanced, fired, loaded, and then advanced again. He lost track of Mr. Turley in the acrid haze that covered the field. A panic started up in him. He was being left behind with the battle raging all around.

Beneath the ringing of the musket shot, Alvin could hear other sounds—low moanings and groanings. A commanding shout rose above the din, and Alvin's line wheeled toward the river. In his rush to keep up, he tripped over a shape that lay sprawled on the ground. He fell, and a whistling zipped past his ear.

Another series of bellowed orders sent the soldiers scattering in all directions. Alvin glanced about through the commotion, and there on his left, where just a half hour before he had marched from under the trees, a swarm of men poured out at a run, naked to the waist, their brown skin stained with slashes of black and red.

Alvin buried his face in the dirt. His mind went numb. Then a scream jerked him up. Not pausing to look for its source, he clambered forward on hands and knees through the snaking smoke of the musket fire. He reached the bank of the river and slithered in. Just a pace downstream, a giant willow had sent out roots to overhang the water. Alvin let himself slip down to the tree, where he wrapped his arms around its roots as best he could.

He was wet and slippery and shaking all over, but still he managed to pull himself up to catch a glimpse of the field. A band of soldiers stumbled through the haze and slid down the riverbank. With nary a look back, they threw themselves into the stream. Alvin searched for his pa in the group, but the smoke was thick, and the splashing water hid their features. The enemy chased up to the bank with muskets firing. A Colonial soldier foundered for a brief moment before he rolled facedown into the current.

Alvin sank back in the shadows. He'd begun to despair for his own escape. Perhaps nightfall and the island that split the waters just across the way would offer shelter. So he waited, shrinking down beneath the willow's roots.

But dusk was a long time coming. Alvin caught a chill, huddled in the water as he was. His teeth commenced to rattle in his head, and when the sun disappeared beyond the hills, taking its last warmth, his insides started to ache. He could wait no longer.

As quietly as he was able, he struck out, keeping low in the water. He swam with short strokes, upstream against the current. He hoped to reach the island before being swept past its downriver end. But the current was swift, and the island shore fled from his outstretched arms. He redoubled his efforts, only to have his muscles rebel. Tears squeezed from his eyes, but when he cried out, the splashing stream filled his mouth.

With a wrenching jerk, he thrust up against a snag that trailed from the island. He clung to the slippery wood, gasped for air, and blessed his luck. Exhausted, he hauled himself ashore to a small, sandy beach. By the time he caught his breath and rested a bit, it was getting full dark, and he began to chill again. Afraid that his shadow would stand out against the light-colored sand of the bank, he scrambled into the underbrush that covered most of the island. And there he found a man sprawled at the foot of a tree, his clothes still wet and a dark stain covering the front of his shirt.

It was Mr. Turley.

Alvin's knees buckled under him, and he sank to the

ground. His heart near stopped from the force of a sudden realization. His pa was still back across the river, somewhere in the middle of the nightmare.

Several moments passed before he could control his shuddering.

"Poor Mr. Turley." He shook his head to clear it of all the terrible possibilities that had lodged there. He pushed himself to his feet.

"You gave me your luck piece," he said, "and plumb ran out of luck yourself."

And then he remembered what Mr. Turley had said: *You can give it back later.*

Alvin pulled the piece out of his vest pocket. Despite the darkness, it flashed silver, reflecting back the stars that appeared overhead. It was a British penny, polished impossibly bright, shining almost white in the gloom.

Alvin placed the coin in Mr. Turley's hand. Then he turned away at the sickness that welled up inside him.

"Boy . . ."

Alvin spun about.

Mr. Turley groaned. "Boy. I don't need the luck no more. Take it back." He tried to reach out but clinched up with pain.

Alvin dropped to his knees at the man's side. "Mr. Turley?"

"Call me Jeremiah."

"Shhh. Don't talk. Rest easy."

"Yes. I'll rest. By a fire. In my own little cabin. I'll rest. For a good, long time."

"You'll be all right. I'll get you to home."

"No . . . I . . . I'm dying." Mr. Turley grabbed Alvin's hand. "Take this. It'll keep you safe." He closed Alvin's fingers around the coin. And then a faint smile spread across his face. "Just a loan," he said. "Just a loan. 'Twas given to me and now to you."

"A loan?"

Mr. Turley's smile turned to a grimace of pain. "Best be on your way."

"I'll keep here with you. We can hide. And come morning—"

"You mustn't," Mr. Turley gasped. "They'll find you. You must get away. Back to the fort. Back to your ma."

"But—"

A musket shot rang across the island and echoed off the far bank.

"Go," Mr. Turley said. "Get away. They're coming."

Alvin hesitated for just an instant, unable to leave the dying man, but loath to stay while the enemy swept through the underbrush.

Mr. Turley waved a hand. "Go!"

Alvin shoved the penny back into his vest pocket. With a single glance over his shoulder, he wriggled rabbitlike through the thicket and headed to the far side of the island. He moved now as fast as he was able, figuring that if he went slow and quiet he'd just be found out anyway.

When he finally slipped into the river, he was able to let the current do most of the work. It pushed him downstream, and his quick strokes sped him across. The water wasn't as wide on this side, and within moments he was scrambling onto the far bank, wet all over again. He took up a driftwood branch for support and staggered away from the river. Movement would keep him warm and take him farther from the nightmare. He eased his breath out, trying to even his labored breathing, but he choked on the next intake.

A single British soldier stood in the darkness, musket held at the ready. "Where are you going?" The soldier stepped forward from the darker gloom of the trees. He was young, along about the age of Alvin's next-oldest brother. "Are you one of those rebels?"

"No, sir." Alvin searched about for an escape. Then an idea struck him, like a flash of silver springing up from his vest pocket.

"I'm loyal to the Crown."

He held up Mr. Turley's luck piece—the penny with the face of King George the Second stamped upon it.

"This here's mine. I don't use none of that rebel money."

The soldier reached for the piece, but as Alvin placed it in his hand, it fell, with a flash, through his fingers. Alvin gasped. The coin seemed to have dropped right through the man's flesh and bone.

The soldier stooped to retrieve it.

Before thinking, Alvin raised the driftwood branch and brought it down with a crack on the soldier's head. Then he snatched up the penny and left the man lying senseless behind him.

Late the next day, shaky with shock and exhaustion, Alvin Corey staggered back into the fort where his ma waited. Together they wept for his pa and two brothers, who never returned from that faraway meadow.

It was many days before Alvin was able to look again at the object of his salvation—a silver penny with the profile of an old dead king. Thoughts of his own father and brothers made him ashamed that trickery and luck had saved him. And then the shame turned to anger. He took the penny and with the sharp corner of a chisel scratched the letters of his defiance over the monarch's name, marking the borrowed coin as his own.

In the middle of the night Deb stirred. Nightmare images jumbled together in his mind, confusing him, mixing up with waking thought. Still groggy, he tried to sort them out, to discover what had made his forehead clammy and his heart pound in his chest. But it was too late. He was waking up. Lydia's baby, Conner, cried from downstairs. The darkness of his dream dissolved into the nighttime shadows of the room.

Conner wailed for a moment, but his cries were muffled as Lydia took to nursing him. Deb listened, and soon there was only silence. He yearned to roll to his side, but his hurt wouldn't allow it. So he kept to his back and tried to remember if there hadn't been anything pleasant in his dreams. He felt drowsy all over again, and his thoughts wandered away. Just as he was dropping off, he jerked awake with a start. Had he heard that ancient, threatening voice again? He reached under the pillow and clutched Grandpa's penny in his fist. A warm reassurance seeped up his arm and into his chest. He finally slipped back to sleep.

Chapter Eleven

*T*AM PEEKED into the barn's gloomy interior. "Grandpa," she called. "Aunt Mary says it's time to eat. Are you in there?" Though not as dark as the root cellar at home, still the barn was full of shadowy nooks and crannies where unseen things could hide. Tam kept to the daylight. She'd had enough of premonitions.

"Grandpa!"

Pigeons chortled from the rafters. Tam pulled the large door full open and let it swing around to bang against the wall. With a whoosh of wings, the startled birds swooped out into the sunshine.

"Are you there?"

Daylight flooded through the open door. Aunt Mary had sent Grandpa to check on Hilde. Since Uncle Arley was busy with the plowing, and Tam's pa and Brady had hitched up the wagon and headed back to home, it was up to Grandpa to see to the young cow, but he was not there. So Tam continued out to the field to call Uncle Arley in, hoping she might find Grandpa along the way. He was nowhere to be seen, not on the open hillside nor between the house and the twin oak trees that grew along the fence.

"Uncle Arley," she called. She climbed up to stand on the bottom rail. Her pa had helped build that fence years ago. And because of Deb, Uncle Arley had just had to repair it. Tam gripped the top rail with both hands, cleared her throat, and called again, "Uncle Arley."

Deb's pa hauled up on the reins. The plow mule shuffled to a stop and dipped her head, seeming glad of the break.

Tam cupped her hands to her mouth and hollered, "It's time to come in." She leaned over the fence, trying to make her voice carry to the middle of the field where Uncle Arley wiped sweat off his forehead with a red handkerchief. "Aunt Mary says it's time to eat."

"Good," he called back. "I was gettin' mighty hungry. I'll just finish this row and leave Jenny to feed in the shade up yonder."

He pulled on his hat and shoved his handkerchief back into his pocket.

"Uncle Arley, have you seen Grandpa? I can't find him anywhere."

"Try the orchard."

Uncle Arley shook the reins and clicked at the mule to get her moving again. Tam hurried to the cow path that slanted across the hillside toward the blossoming trees. She found Grandpa on the far side of the orchard, where the path dipped down through the meandering creek. He was bent over, preoccupied with something that lay on the bank.

"Grandpa, there you are!"

"Shhhh," he hissed. Then he mouthed the words "come here."

Tam followed his curious instructions and drew near, holding up her skirt to keep it from catching on the new-grown thistle that edged the path.

"What is it?"

Grandpa hushed her with his hand.

"Looky here what I found." He nodded at the figure that leaned against a weatherworn stump. "What do you reckon it is?"

"Grandpa, it's that boy."

A while later, Tam rushed up the stairs into the loft to tell Deb the news, but she tripped on the top step and fell to the floor in a tangle of gingham and legs. She jumped up and smoothed her skirt back down over her pantaloons.

Deb stared at her.

"Mind if I come in?" she asked.

"Seems you already have."

"You're looking much better today." She hoped he wouldn't mind the lie.

Deb shrugged.

"Aunt Mary says you can come down soon. Uncle Arley's going to make a place for you to sit on the porch. It smells so good and fine out there." She wrinkled up her nose. "Not like in here."

"I don't smell anything," Deb said. "'Sides, there isn't anything fine about watching you folks just walk around."

"The flowers are all blooming. Aunt Mary's crocuses are gone, but the flags are out in the meadow. And my mama's lilac she planted when I was born is just blossoming. And there's a new hummingbird that came this morning. Deb, you'll be able to see the rest of spring." She couldn't help the gush of words.

Deb shrugged again. "I've seen flowers."

"But it's spring. We could go down to the creek and catch toads and frogs and—"

She stopped at the sour look on Deb's face.

"I'm sorry," she said. "I forgot. But at least you could come out and see the boy."

"Boy? What boy?"

"I think he's a half-wit. We saw him on the road yesterday, fast asleep like never-you-please—like his own bedroom was the great, wide out-of-doors."

"On the road? Now how would *I* get clear out *there?*"

She set her hands on her hips. "Weren't you listening? He isn't there. He's here. Grandpa found him. Out by the orchard, near the stream. He was asleep, just like yesterday. Only this time, he didn't run away when Grandpa woke him. He stayed put right where he was with a silly grin on his face. I think he must have smelled dinner."

"Who is he? Where'd he come from?"

"He's a simpleton. He has hardly any clothes on, just a raggedy old pair of overalls. No shoes at all—and no shirt, neither. Aunt Mary's feeding him dinner. He doesn't have very good manners. He's a pig. Worse than you."

"What do you mean, worse than me? I can't help—"

"Oh, Deb. I'm sorry. I was just teasing. I didn't mean anything about . . . well, you know."

She couldn't think of anything else to say. Her news

didn't seem to be of any comfort to her cousin, not even the idea of his getting out into the fresh spring air.

"Well, I better get back down there in case your ma needs my help cleaning up after that boy."

Deb just nodded, then turned to stare out the window again.

When Tam stepped out on the porch, Aunt Mary handed another plate of food to the stranger-boy and stood back. She didn't seem much concerned with his lack of manners. She just watched while he shoveled the steaming stew into his mouth, using only a flat knife and a hunk of bread as tools.

"His name is Bray Skoolle," Aunt Mary said. "Poor thing. Seems he hasn't eaten in days. He couldn't say where his family is."

"Maybe he doesn't have one," Tam whispered. "Maybe he's an orphan. A nitwit boy that nobody wanted."

"*Hst.* Tam! That was uncalled for. Where are your manners?"

Aunt Mary's rebuke stung. Tam hung her head, letting the red embarrassment creep up to her ears. "I'm sorry," she mumbled to the floor. She almost added, "I didn't mean it," but that would have been a lie. She still begrudged the boy his laughter of the day before, and now with Aunt Mary's anger heaped upon her, she further sharpened her contrary opinion of him.

Through lowered eyes, she watched his bobbing thatch of red hair, but try as she might, she couldn't see any of the signs of idiocy she claimed for him. Instead, he had an impish, almost clever air. His gaze darted about even while he ate, gathering in the farmhouse, the barn, the orchard and fields. Finally his searching eyes rested on Tam, and he grinned.

"Thank'ee for the water yesterday," he said, the lilt high in his voice. "'Twas pleasant after the long nap."

Tam nodded and then remembered. "You never drank!"

"Naw, but it's the thought that counts."

He finished sopping up the gravy with the last of the bread, took a final drink, and handed Aunt Mary the plate, knife, and cup.

"Thank'ee, ma'am, for the dinner. I've not tasted food like that for a long time."

"Why, you're welcome, Mr. Skoolle. And you're welcome to stay the night, if you've a mind to."

"Thank'ee, ma'am. Maybe I will."

Later that evening Tam stood on the porch with extra bedding clutched in her arms. Though the sun was well gone and stars were already peeking out, the night was not completely dark, for the rising moon was barely past her full. Tam shivered in the cool air. It would be a quick errand, she told herself. Just a dash across the shadowed yard and back before her fear of the dark had a chance to snatch at her. She had reflected on telling Aunt Mary no, that she didn't want to do any favors for that boy, but that would've only made matters worse.

A lantern inside the barn painted a half circle of feeble light on the ground at the open door. Tam stepped down from the porch and scurried across the yard, holding her bundle so that none of it would drag in the dirt. She stopped just outside the barn, her curiosity making her pause to listen to what sounded like singing. She peeked inside. The lantern was just dim enough that she had to scan the dusky interior twice before she understood what she was seeing.

The boy, Bray, had draped himself over the back of the cow in her stall, his arms dangling around her neck, his head resting on her tawny shoulder. And he was singing to her. Humming a lullaby song, sweet and low, as if to a child. Maybe she had been right all along. Perhaps there was something wrong with this boy.

"Hello?" she said.

Bray looked up and smiled. "She'll be calvin' soon.

Within the week. But have a care. The wee one's a bit turned about."

"Aunt Mary sent some extra blankets for you. In case it chills tonight."

"Thank'ee. But the hay should be plenty warm."

"Aunt Mary said you could come into the house and sleep there. We can make up a bed."

"Naw, this is just fine for me."

"You don't have to stay in the barn."

"I wouldn't know what to do with a bed," he said.

"All right." Tam couldn't say why exactly, but it did seem he would be more comfortable here. "How do you know the calf will be so soon?"

"Oh, look at her. She's set to bust. Within the week."

Tam put the pile of blankets down and turned to go.

"Wait a bit," Bray called to her. He slid off Hilde and climbed out of the stall.

"What is it?" Her question sounded more snappish than she had wished.

"I'm awful sorry," he said.

"What for?" Though she asked, she could think of several things he should be sorry for. Perhaps he was going to apologize for laughing at her yesterday. Apologize for the anger and embarrassment he had put her through today. She shook her head as if she couldn't guess what it was all about. "Whatever for?" she asked again, putting a flippant, unconcerned tone in her voice.

"I'm sorry your cousin is hurt so bad."

"Oh." That wasn't what she expected. "Thank you."

"You're welcome. But things often get worse 'fore they get any better."

Chapter Twelve

DEB LEANED BACK on the couch Pa had set up for him on the porch. After being stuck inside for so long, the warm afternoon sunshine felt good on his face. Tam had been right about the spring air and flowers, but the pleasure of it all was not much comfort. Grandpa's hex hadn't worked near well enough. Though it kept him homebound, the ache in his heart to wander away burned stronger than ever. The only thing that seemed to make him feel any better was Grandpa's silver penny, kept hidden upstairs under his pillow so Ma wouldn't find it.

Looking at the yard, he remembered the dream he'd had in his sickness—the dream of the crooked old man drawing a circle around him in the dirt. Even now, it seemed more real than a dream, and its memory made him shiver. He wondered if maybe he should have smuggled the penny down with him. But if Ma saw it . . .

Deb shifted on his makeshift couch, trying to ease the fatigue of his backside. He'd been sitting there since morning while the daily chores of the farm passed about him. Ma had even brought out his midday meal, since he couldn't sit proper at the table.

Out beyond the fence Pa was almost done turning the soil and would soon be planting, pushing his shovel into the ground and dropping in a fistful of seed corn. Ma was inside, scrubbing down the walls and cleaning the lamp-soot off the woodwork and trim. From out back came a thump-thumping, as Lydia beat the winter dust from the blankets and bedding. And Deb could hear someone stacking wood in the shed on the far side of the house.

Tam struggled toward the barn with a heavy wooden bucket. Water sloshed on her skirt and shoes. She set the bucket down and flexed her hands, then waved at Deb.

"Still in your nightshirt?" she called.

Deb grimaced at her, then looked out to the field. The hawk was there again, perched on the new fence post Pa had just replaced.

"Shoo that thing out of here," he yelled to Tam. "Scare it away."

Tam followed Deb's pointing finger. "He's not hurting anything."

"It's after the chickens. Scare it away."

Tam shrugged. Then she ran after the bird, waving her arms and whooping.

The startled hawk swept across the yard and into the orchard.

Tam went back to her bucket, but before she could pick it up, the red-haired stranger-boy appeared from inside the barn. He wrapped both hands around the bucket's handle and turned to Tam as if awaiting instructions.

With a glance at Deb, she pointed into the dark interior of the barn. "For Hilde," Deb heard her say.

Tam was giggling when the two came back into daylight.

"Helpful little fellow," Grandpa said.

"Grandpa! I didn't see you come around."

"Sorry. Didn't mean to startle you." Grandpa stood near the porch, wiping his hands on his handkerchief. He nodded toward the barn. "I guess she's gotten over her dislike of the boy."

"Well, he is doing her chores."

"He's mighty obliging all right. You know, there's something about him—"

"I think he's troublesome."

"No . . . that's not it." Grandpa climbed the steps onto the porch. "It'll come to me what it is. But right now, I think I'm gonna take me a bit of a rest."

"Already? What time is it?"

Grandpa peered in through the open door at the old clock on the fireplace mantel. "Near on to two o'clock, and here I am, already done with all my chores." He nodded again toward the barn. "And that boy did most of 'em. I went out to sharpen the ax so it would be ready for your pa, but the grinder was already wet, and the ax shiny and sharp enough to cut shadows. And there he was, stackin' wood."

Deb scowled at the boy and his cousin as they wandered off toward the orchard. "How long you think Ma's gonna let him stay?" he asked. But Grandpa had already disappeared into the house.

That evening after supper, Pa carried Deb up to fresh bedding and an aired-out room. Between the two of them they were able to wriggle Deb into a clean nightshirt. It was still light out, though the sun had already begun its dip toward nighttime. The spring evening had turned into the warmest yet of the year. Deb lay back on his bed with the covers pulled down and his legs stretched out before him.

"It's hot," he said.

He eased the nightshirt up above his knees and sighted, squint-eye, down each leg, comparing one against the other. From that vantage, the difference between the two was insignificant, the one on the right showing its injury in just a slight twisting of the foot.

"Look, Pa," he said, "I think it's gonna straighten out."

"Yep," Pa answered. "You'll prove that old doctor wrong. You'll be up and about in no time at all."

"You think before the summer's over?"

"Maybe."

"I hope so. I don't want to spend all summer just sitting around."

Pa stroked his mustache, smoothing it down while he looked at Deb. "You know, I seem to remember a boy complaining, once upon a time, about all the work he had to do around here."

"I think even chores would be an excitement now."

"You reckon?"

"Yeh, I reckon."

Pa tousled Deb's hair. "You get your rest, then, and just let that body mend itself. You'll have your fill of chores soon enough."

"Well, I've had my fill of bed, and that's the truth. I think I'll even sleep standing up from now on. One thing that's good from all this, though."

"What's that?"

"No birthday whippings."

"Oh, you think not? Maybe they'll just have to wait till you're better. Or do you figure you've been good enough to get out of it this year?"

"Now that you mention it . . ."

"Seems to me there's the matter of the horse and the fence."

Throughout Pa's cheerful banter, Deb had been right on the verge of good feelings. Now, even though the room around him was still bright with the evening light, he felt a twinge of darkness inside, thinking of poor old Betsy. "I'm sorry," he whispered.

Pa's smile faded away. "Son, I'm sorry, too. I reckon that was a bad jest. You've had punishment enough. Now cheer up. You may not get your birthday whippin's, but we're surely gonna have a celebration."

Pa's attempt at cheerfulness didn't half work. Deb continued to stare down at his leg, thinking it would be fitting if he never walked again. Betsy had been old but still of faithful use to the family—not easily replaced. And here was Pa, talking about a celebration.

Pa turned to the stairs and almost collided with Tam as she rushed into the room.

She caught herself up short. "Uncle Arley." Her voice was breathless from running. "Grandpa needs your help."

"What's he up to now?"

"Fixing the apple press."

Pa rolled his eyes to the ceiling. "I better get right out there." He hurried down the stairs.

Tam turned to Deb, her eyes bright in the evening light. "Everything was going fine until the hopper fell off." And then she giggled. "First time I ever heard Grandpa cuss." She ran a hand along the edge of Deb's bed. Her look sobered as she stared down at his exposed leg.

Feeling self-conscious, Deb tried to push his night-shirt back into place. Tam reached out and tugged it down for him, covering his knees.

"Does it still hurt?" she asked.

"Not much."

"It looks awful. All twisted up. How's it ever gonna straighten out for you to walk?"

Deb examined his leg again, leaning as far forward as he was able. "What do you mean? It's looking lots better."

"Oh." Tam fidgeted with her skirt for a bit. "Well, I better go see if they need any help." She left in a hurry.

Deb's eyes blurred. He compared the two legs again, this time with Tam's words weighing heavy in his judg-ment. At last he laid back on his pillow and watched the evening disappear against the slanted ceiling of his room.

Sometime later Tam returned, bearing a lamp—a flickering light that preceded her up the stairs. "You asleep?" she whispered.

"Nuh-uh."

"How are you feeling?"

"All right. Did the press get fixed?"

"Was all done by the time your pa got there."

"Grandpa was able to lift the hopper back up by himself?"

"No. It was that boy, Bray. By the time we got out there, he had the whole thing back together, working fine."

Deb looked again at the slanted roof. Rough-hewn crossbeams cast wavering shadows as the light from Tam's lamp flickered up against them.

"He's still here?" he asked.

"Your ma said he's welcome to stay. She said with the way he helps around here, he could stay as long as he wanted."

"Maybe if I could get up she wouldn't need the help."

"Well, your pa is going to make a crutch for you," Tam offered. "Then you will be able to get up."

"I still can't do nothin'!" Deb hadn't meant to yell, but

it was too late to call it back. He turned his head so he wouldn't have to watch the smile drop from his cousin's face.

The creak on the stairs and the fading light were the only indication she was gone. Right outside the open window Deb could hear the hoot of an owl. With a sudden desperation, he reached a hand under his pillow. But Ma had changed his bedding just that afternoon. The silver penny was gone.

Chapter Thirteen

SOMETIME in the middle of the night, Tam roused in a panic, scared awake by nightmare visions of Deb lying helpless alongside a dusty road, his leg bruised and twisted beneath him. She opened her eyes to the darkness of the great room, but her bad dreams still lurked in the inky shadows. She pulled the blankets up to her chin, aware now of a strange sound that creaked across the room. She held her breath and listened. From somewhere came the steady squeak of wood on wood. Straining to hear, she tried to convince herself that it couldn't be the rocking chair by the fireplace—that it was only the nighttime settling of the old farmhouse. But the noise was too regular, as if the chair were rocking, empty and alone in the darkness. She pulled the covers past her nose. She didn't even dare a peek across the room.

"Lydia," she whispered, "are you awake?"

Lydia had always been a light sleeper, but it seemed that now, with the baby, she slept through everything but his noise. The frightful sound continued, growing louder with each sliding creak.

"Lydia!"

Her cousin's groggy voice answered from the bed. "What . . . what is it?"

"Who's in the rocking chair?"

"What?"

"Someone's in the rocking chair. Can you see?"

"Tam, go back to sleep. No one's there."

"But can't you hear it?"

"Hear what?"

"The rocking chair. By the fireplace. It's moving."

"No, it's not."

"Then what's that sound?"

"What sound?"

"Listen. That sound."

"Tam, that's just the clock ticking. Go back to sleep. The baby'll be waking soon. Let me get some rest." Lydia's head fell back to her pillow.

"The clock?"

"Yes, dear."

Tam listened as the ominous sound faded into the harmless ticking of the old timepiece. Its rhythmic creaking beat out the seconds from its place on the mantel. Braving a look, she peered through the darkness to the far side of the room. The rocking chair sat still and silent in its accustomed place by the hearth.

Tam fell back to her pillow, embarrassed at her foolishness. But as she lay there fretting about what Lydia might be thinking, a realization struck her. The chair, after all, was only a chair. Deb would always be Deb, whether his broken leg mended or not.

"Lydia?"

"Yes?"

Tam could hear the *"what now?"* in the reply. "Will Deb's leg straighten out so he can walk at all?"

Lydia didn't answer right away, giving Tam time to begin her wondering all over again.

"Yes, of course," Lydia finally said.

Tam tried to believe her cousin, but it was hard, surrounded by the shadowy darkness. She lay still and listened to the clock ticking, wondering how she ever could have thought it sounded like a rocking chair.

The next morning Tam leaned upon the breakfast table in a daze. She ate little and only nodded to Grandpa's cheerfulness.

"Still asleep?" he asked.

"She had a difficult night," Lydia said. She smiled and excused herself to tend to the baby.

"Guilty conscience?" Grandpa asked.

Uncle Arley stood and stamped into his boots. "Now, what would she have to be guilty about?"

Tam yawned. "I was just worried about Deb."

"Don't you worry about your cousin," Aunt Mary said. "He's going to be just fine." She stacked the breakfast plates and carried them to the washtub. Tam pushed herself up to help.

"But isn't he coming down today?"

Aunt Mary shook her head. "He says he's tired and wants to stay upstairs."

"Is he all right? Is he getting sick again?"

"No, dear. I think he just feels a little low today."

"Low?" Tam glanced out the window at the bright morning. Though she was tired and out of sorts from the fitful night, she couldn't understand how anyone could be low on such a day. "Is there anything I can do to cheer him up?"

"Tomorrow's his birthday. That will help."

"I think he's just tired of all this fuss," Grandpa said. "And tired of not being able to get around so well."

"I guess I'd get tired of being in bed all day, too. But I sure wouldn't mind watching somebody else do my chores."

"You reckon so?" Grandpa asked.

"Well . . . as long as they did them right."

"Yes, and speaking of chores . . ." Aunt Mary glanced at the door.

"I know," Tam said. "Hilde."

"And don't forget to water her."

"Yes, ma'am."

Tam stepped out onto the porch. Despite the heaviness that still lodged behind her eyes, the sun-fresh coolness felt pleasant on her skin. She sniffed the air and let the whole of springtime compete for her attention. She fancied she could pick out each smell in its turn. She noticed, as if for the first time, the yellow-headed dandelions that spread their color over the grass in haphazard clusters.

With all of spring gathered around, the fatigue that bothered her dissolved into an agreeable drowsiness. She crossed to the barn and entered its gloomy interior, feeling braver about the shadows. Somehow, the stranger-boy's presence had served to make the barn safe.

"Bray?" she called.

Earlier Uncle Arley had brought a plate of breakfast out to the boy, respecting his bashfulness of the house, but had been unable to find him. Tam found the plate, wiped clean and sitting on a hogshead just inside the door.

"Bra-ay."

There was no answer.

Anxious to finish her work and get back out into sunlight, she grabbed the pitchfork and scooped it up with hay. Then she realized Hilde's manger was already full and her tub brimming with water.

Tam shook her head. "That boy." She climbed up on Hilde's stall and stroked the cow's back. "Now where'd he get to, huh?"

Hilde pulled up another mouthful of hay, ignoring Tam's question to concentrate on her chewing. Tam rested her head on the top rail of the stall and watched as the cow continued her leisurely feeding. A pleasant dimness settled into Tam's sight, making her eyelids feel heavy and dull. Hilde's methodic chewing hypnotized her with its slow sideways motion and crunching sound. Hanging on that railing, Tam nearly dropped off to sleep, but a sound from behind startled her.

"Oh, it's you," she said.

Bray was leaning against the barn door. "You'd do better to sleep at night," he said, "'stead a lying awake, frettin' 'bout things you cannot change."

Chapter Fourteen

*D*ON'T WORRY, SON," Grandpa said. "It'll turn up."

Deb fretted at the blankets with his hands. "Ma must have shook it out with the bedding. Do you think it could be down in the yard?"

"I reckon."

"Or under the bed? Can you see it? Is it there?" Deb leaned out as far as he was able and tried to peek over the side. He had a sinking feeling that with the penny gone, so was any luck he had left.

Grandpa bent down with a hand on his knee and tried to peer under the draped blankets. Deb pulled on the covers to lift them up out of Grandpa's way.

"I'll get Tam to come give a look," Grandpa said. "It'll turn up."

"If it got shook out in the yard, it could be lost for-ever."

"Now son, don't worry none. I reckon we'll find it. Always have. Why, once it was lost for a whole year."

"A whole year?"

"Yep. Or thereabouts."

Grandpa eased himself down into the rocking chair. "Deb," he said, "I've got to tell you, there's something mighty peculiar about that coin. I know I've filled your head with ridiculous notions of magic and charms, but that coin *is* different. When poor Mr. Turley told me it would keep me safe, he wasn't saying it just to comfort me."

"What do you mean?"

"I mean, without it I wouldn't be here. And I don't just mean that little set-to with the redcoats."

"But . . . but you said you lost it."

"Yup, it was lost. And then it came back, just like that."

Grandpa pulled his handkerchief out of his pocket and wiped his nose.

"Yup," he said, "just like that. It happened when your pa was little. That coin just disappeared one day. I couldn't find it nowhere. Then, some while later— maybe a year—I was working in the gristmill with my boy Joseph, your pa's pa. We was grinding up our own share of grain. It was hot, sticky work. I took out my handkerchief, like I did just now, to wipe the dust off my face, and that penny dropped down on the floor like it fell out from the sky. When I bent over to pick it up, I heard a great cracking sound, like a cannon shot. Next thing I knew I was buried in a mountain of grain. There was so much of it I couldn't move. It was an awful feeling, being pushed down under all that weight—like my body was split in two, my thinking part going one way and my feeling part going the other. I knew I was done for. But just as the parts of me began to wander off to someplace else, old Jack Walker reached in and pulled me back.

"Jack ran the mill in those days. He was a good man. He's dead now." Grandpa wiped his nose again and then looked hard at Deb. "Though it was Jack pulled me out, it was the penny that saved me."

"The penny saved you? How?"

"Well, old Jack said he panicked when he saw what had happened, 'cause he didn't even know where to look for me. But then he saw a glint of silver in the grain and took it for a sign of where to dig.

"It was that penny he saw. It must have been knocked out of my hand by the avalanche. And there it lay for Jack to find. So it was lost for a year, right there in my own pocket, I reckon. And found just in time."

The old man's account was already familiar to Deb. "My grandpa Joseph was killed in that collapse, wasn't he? You've told me that story before, but you never said anything about the penny. Why not?"

Grandpa shrugged his shoulders. "I guess it always troubled me that my lucky piece was able to save me and not my boy."

"We gotta find it," Deb said. "Maybe—maybe it'll help me to walk."

Grandpa shook his head. "Now, son, don't go placing your hopes on something like that. Luck comes and goes when it will. What you need is rest and good doctoring."

"Will you find it anyway?"

"Course. I'll try."

Grandpa paused and searched Deb's eyes, as if he were looking for something there. "Son," he said, "though we keep on saying that everything will be fine, that your leg will mend good as new, that you'll be up and around in no time, you've got to realize . . . well . . . that things don't always work out the way we want. You understand?"

"Yes, I understand. But please find me that penny."

Once Deb was sure that Grandpa had descended the stairs out of hearing, he threw back his covers and struggled against the feather tick, pushing himself with his good leg until he sat at the edge of the bed. With a grimace, he slid to the floor and balanced on one foot. He felt light-headed from the exertion, but even with his injury he was more limber than Grandpa. He bent down to search the dusty shadows under his bed.

"Looking for something?"

Deb started. Bray Skoolle stood at the top of the stairs.

"I lost something, too," the redheaded boy said. "But 'twas a long time ago."

"What are you doing in my room?"

"Wouldn't it be peculiar if we both lost the same thing?"

"No!"

Bray laughed. "I expect you're right." And then he sobered. "There's a saying my folk have—sometimes you have to get lost yourself to find the thing you're looking for. I dunno. Seems bleak to me."

Deb tried to pull himself up on the bed, to get back under the covers.

"Here, let me help," Bray said.

"No. I can do."

Deb squirmed onto the bed, blowing his breath out through his teeth. With a final grunt he rolled to his back and let his head fall on the pillow. "I can do," he whispered to the ceiling.

When he looked up, Bray was gone.

Next day at first light, Tam bounded into Deb's room and swept across the floor with a cheerful noise that made him cringe.

> *You are twelve years old today,*
> *And I'm glad to hear them say,*
> *That you cannot be the baby anymore.*

She finished her song with a clap of hands that echoed in the morning air.

Deb frowned at her merriment. He pulled the blankets over his head. "Let me sleep."

"Come on, slugabed," Tam insisted. "It's your birthday."

"Go away." He wished he could roll to his side and bury his head in the pillow.

"Oh, please. It's a beautiful day."

Deb didn't answer. From under his covers, he could hear the swish of Tam's skirt.

"Well, I guess you can just come down when you want," she finally said. She clattered back to the stairs.

"No I can't," he whispered to himself.

It wasn't until midmorning that Deb called out to be carried down to the porch. He had to holler as loud as he was able before Ma came up the stairs, shaking her head.

"What is it now?" she asked from the top step, her hands white with flour and her hair wisped out around her face.

"I want to come down now."

"You'll have to wait till noontime, when Pa comes in for his meal."

"But, Ma, where is everybody?"

"Out and about, taking care of things." She turned back to the stairs.

"Tell Grandpa I want to ask him something."

She paused. "Now, what do you need from Grandpa? He's busy, too."

"Oh. . . . Nothing, I guess."

"Fine."

Deb sighed at the exasperation in her voice. "I'm sorry," he said as she descended out of sight.

A few moments later he heard a commotion from the foot of the stairs. He recognized Tam's giggle and could picture her trying to hide her laughter behind cupped hands. He yearned to know what the joke was about, to bound down the stairs and throw himself into the middle of the fracas.

But the noise of it tumbled up the stairs to him. Tam rushed into the loft, pulling Bray Skoolle behind her.

"Deb, you'll never guess what he made for you."

Deb tugged the covers up to his chest. "What do you want?"

"Bray made you a birthday present."

The boy hung back, but there was a sparkle in his eyes that filled Deb with resentment.

"What do you want?" he asked again.

"Since you wouldn't come down," Tam said, "we thought we'd bring it up to you."

"What?" Deb craned his neck, trying to see what Bray had hidden behind him.

Tam shoved Bray toward the bed.

"Your pa won't need to make a crutch for you after all," she said. "Look."

At her prompting, Bray held out an object carved from apple wood. It was made from a single branch, whittled clean.

"Isn't it wonderful? Look how he's carved it. See, your name, 'Jacob Corey.' He polished it up real good. Made the padding out of lamb's wool. And look here—"

"Tam! Stop your jabberin'." Deb scowled at his cousin.

He turned to Bray. "I don't need nothin' from you. Why don't you all just let me be?"

"But, Deb," Tam pleaded.

"Just leave me alone!"

With a jerk of his head, Deb dismissed the tears that had started up in his cousin's eyes. "Go on! Get out of here." And then he turned his face to the wall.

They left him without a sound. When he looked back to where they had stood, he saw the crutch laid across the foot of the bed. He kicked at it, and it fell clattering to the floor.

Chapter Fifteen

*T*HE CREEK CHATTERED along, sparkling bright in its springtime rush. Tam sat on its bank and plunged her feet into the cold water. She dug her toes into the pebbles and sand of the creek bed to stir up a murky dust that was pulled away by the current. She plucked at the new shoots of grass that edged the bank.

Someone called her name. Lydia. But Tam wasn't ready to be found, so she left the call unanswered. She wiped her eyes with the back of her hand.

"Drat Deb!" She threw a handful of grass into the tumbling water. The blades scattered over the surface and hurried downstream.

The cold made her ankles ache, so she pulled her feet

out of the stream and folded her legs beneath her, drying them within her skirt.

A shuffling step from behind startled her. "Grandpa! Where'd you come from?"

"Pretty day," he said as he stepped down the path toward the creek.

Tam grunted.

"Nice day for a walk."

"It's too close to noon," she said. "We'll be eating soon."

"May I sit with you then?"

"Lydia was calling me."

"She can wait. Tam, I just wanted to talk a bit."

"What about?"

Grandpa shrugged his shoulders. "Your cousin. Don't go being hurt by anything Deb says. He's not himself. He doesn't mean—"

"Grandpa, he was just plain rude." She gathered up her shoes and stockings. "I better go see what Lydia was wanting."

She hurried past Grandpa and on up the orchard path toward the house. But once under the shade of the overspreading branches, she left the path and wound her way through the trees themselves. She wandered aimlessly, pulling at an occasional leaf or kicking at a clump of new orchard grass with her bare feet.

"Drat Deb!"

But then she stopped and listened.

A kind of song floated through the shadows beneath the branches—a melancholy song that seemed to push at her belligerent mood. Curious, she picked her way through the trees toward the small clearing that Grandpa had used to burn years of prunings. There she saw Bray, sitting on his knees in the center of the empty space.

She hid behind a tree to watch.

The redheaded boy seemed oblivious to the orchard around him, his attention fixed instead on the ground at his knees. He was singing a song so foreign that Tam couldn't make out where one word left off and another began. Though it seemed a nonsense song, the grace of it melted her anger and hurt clean away.

She looked closer at what held the boy's attention. A pile of small sticks and twigs had been arranged on the ground before him. As he sang, he pulled a twig from a bundle in his fist and placed it on the pile.

Tam crept from behind the tree. Bray glanced up and caught her eyes in his. A smile spread over his face.

"Hello," he said.

"What are you doing?" Tam moved out into the sunshine. The warmth was pleasant on her skin.

"Ever the curious one, eh?" Bray said.

"What were those words? Did you make them up? I didn't recognize a one. Is . . . is it magic?"

Bray ignored her questions. "This is an uncommon place. Your grandpa was wise not to plant trees here."

"How did you know Grandpa planted these trees?"

"It's an old orchard. He's an old man. Who else?"

Tam shrugged. "No one, I guess. But you're sitting right in the ashes. Grandpa burns the prunings here."

Bray fell to his back. "They're apple ashes. How could they harm me?"

"You're getting awful dirty."

"Dirt grows the trees. How could it be awful?"

He sat up again, careful of the pile of sticks he had built. "This is a good place for thinking."

"Thinking about what?"

"Things." He grew quiet.

"Bray? Are you still angry at Deb? Grandpa says he didn't mean—"

"Oh, but he did. And I never was angry with him. The truth is he likely won't walk again. Not without trouble. And it hurts him, worse than the hurt in his leg."

Tam let her gaze drop down to the pile of sticks. She shook her head but the tears came anyway, falling into the gray dust at her feet. Bray stood and, with a brief touch on her shoulder, walked back toward the house, leaving her alone in the center of Grandpa's burning place.

When they all sat down to the midday meal that noon, Bray sat with them for the first time. Aunt Mary seemed pleased that he had finally accepted her invitation. Tam noticed, however, that he wasn't eating. Instead he looked about the family with a curious gaze. When he became aware of Tam's eyes upon him, he grinned, scooped up a bite of food, and shoveled it into his mouth.

After the meal was cleared away, Aunt Mary sent Tam out to check on Hilde. She passed Deb on the porch, where he had been carried to eat his meal. He was still unable to sit at the table, so Arley had brought him down to the couch, and Lydia had taken a plate of food out to him.

Tam offered him a weak smile, hoping that he might at least feel better in his heart. Perhaps the birthday celebration this evening would cheer him up. He ignored her smile and looked away. She tried to remember Bray's words and not hold Deb's manner against him. But it was hard to disregard the feeling in her own heart. She walked across the yard with her head lowered.

Halfway to the barn, however, she forgot her own troubles when she heard the cow's bawling from inside the open door.

"The wee one's on its way," Bray said from behind.

They ran the rest of the way together. Hilde was down in her stall, forelegs tucked beneath, hind legs sprawled out behind.

"She's begun," Bray said. "Best get Uncle Arley. It's going to be a difficult birthing." He knelt down beside Hilde and stroked her side. "It's hard to push a wee one out into this world only to let it go on to the next."

He looked up at Tam. "Go! Get your uncle. He'll be needed for more than this."

Tam rushed out of the barn, her skirt flying as she ran toward the field to fetch Uncle Arley. He had just begun planting on a new row.

She hollered over the fence to him, "It's Hilde. The calf is coming."

Arley booted his shovel into the soft earth and left it standing at an angle. He walked easily over the rows, judging his steps to miss the already planted grain.

"She look all right?" he asked.

"I think so. Bray's with her now. But he said—"

"I'll just come have a look."

Chapter Sixteen

WHILE TAM and Bray hurried toward the barn, Deb kept his gaze fixed on a patch of ground before the porch. He squinted at the small, shiny object that winked up through the grass and dandelions, but it was too far off to be sure. He considered the distance to the object. He tried to convince himself the stretch was possible.

The stairs would be the hard part.

He put his good foot down on the porch and tried to grip onto it with his toes. He lifted his injured leg with both hands and brought it around to the edge of the couch. The crutch the stranger-boy had made would have been useful, but it was still lying on the floor at the foot of his bed. The post of the porch would have to be support enough. He pulled himself to standing, then balanced with a hand on the post. His right leg hung crooked and useless.

"Just wait," he whispered to it. "I'll have that penny."

A shuffling hop brought him to the top of the stairs. There he hesitated, scanning the yard. Bray Skoolle stood just inside the barn door looking out at him. Tam was away off at the field. Deb puffed his breath out through clenched teeth and gave another hop, but in his hurry, his injured foot dragged on the top step.

A shock of pain flashed up his leg. He flailed his arms, but that sent him farther off balance. Clutching for the post, he let out a cry and lost his footing altogether.

He heard a popping sound as he crashed down into the yard. The pain rushed through his whole body. He tore up a handful of grass and tried to will the hurt away into the brown-patterned darkness that seeped into his vision. He rolled to his back, blinking at the searing light of the afternoon sun.

"I'll help," he heard a voice say.

"I can do," Deb groaned in return.

He pushed himself to his hands and knees, struggling against the pinpricks that crawled all over him. From a distance he heard a scream. *Tam,* he thought. He felt a pulling at his leg, dragging him into darkness. He squeezed at the silver penny he'd clutched along with the fistful of grass. But this time the monster's grip was too much. Deb no longer had the will to fight.

Chapter Seventeen

*T*AM WATCHED through streaming tears as Uncle Arley carried Deb inside. She stood in the yard and pulled at her apron hem with trembling hands.

"Is he dead?" she whispered to Grandpa.

The old man's response was barely audible. "No." But Tam could see the worry in his face.

Uncle Arley rushed back out of the house. "I'm going for Doc Williams," he said, leaping down the steps.

Tam was torn between looking after Deb and the fear of what she might see.

Arley led the mule out of the barn and jumped up on her back. "Take care of Hilde," he called. "She's gonna need help. The calf is coming breech." He kicked at the mule, urging her out the gate and down the road.

"Mary and Lydia'll watch over the boy," Grandpa said. "We best get out to the barn."

"I'll help," Bray said. The impish look had disappeared from his face, replaced by a gravity Tam had not seen there before.

They hurried to the barn.

"What can I do?" Tam asked.

"Hilde can't push enough," Grandpa said. "We'll need to pull."

The three of them set to work. Together they struggled with the calf, trying to maneuver it, hind feet first, through the birth canal.

"Why's it so hard?" Tam asked. In her mind, the calf's bony hindquarters should be easier to deliver than his big head.

"The wee one's coat grows to the back," Bray answered. "Coming shoulder first, the nap is smooth. Backwards and the nap turns rough. He can't slide out clean."

"And his legs don't fold the right way," Grandpa said. "Why, I seen men use a rope and a horse to pull 'em out this way afore. Too bad we don't have Betsy here to help."

To Tam it seemed the calf would never come free.

"It's taking too long," Bray said after what seemed ages.

Grandpa took a deep breath. "It is."

"What is? What's wrong?" Tam didn't know whether

they were talking about Uncle Arley's search for the doctor or the calf's delivery.

"We've gotta get the little feller out," Grandpa said, "or we'll lose Hilde, too."

"We just have to work harder," Bray said.

Tam dug her knees into the straw and braced herself the best she could. Once again they took hold of the calf's legs and pulled with all their strength. Tam could feel her heart pounding through her head with the strain. Hilde was no longer bawling like before. She seemed exhausted herself.

At long last the calf slipped free of its mother in a rush of bloody fluid. The newborn lay still in the straw.

Grandpa put a hand to his back and tried to straighten up. "At least we've saved Hilde."

"'Tis a fair exchange," Bray said, pushing the hair up off his face with his blood-smeared forearm.

Tam tried hard not to cry. Then she remembered Deb lying in the house, and the tears sprang to her eyes before she could stop them.

It was evening when Uncle Arley finally arrived with Doc Williams. They rolled up to the house in a buggy with the mule trotting behind. The doc jumped down and left Arley to see to the rig.

Aunt Mary led the doc into the house to her own

bedroom, where Deb had been laid. Tam and Grandpa followed close behind. Doc Williams made a cursory examination, counting Deb's heartbeat and pushing open his eyelids to peer into his eyes.

"Cold water," he said.

Lydia hurried from the room.

"What can I do?" Tam asked.

"Towels."

Tam hurried into the kitchen just as Lydia returned with a basin of water.

"It's mighty dangerous," Tam heard the doc say as she brought in a stack of folded towels. "His leg will need to be reset. The shock of it—Uh, thank you, girl." He nodded to Tam and began to bathe Deb's head and face with a towel dampened with cool water.

When Doc Williams left late that night, Deb was still lying senseless on the bed. His breathing came thin and shallow, and his skin was a dull, pasty color. Though the leg had been reset and wrapped with a clean bandage, he remained unconscious.

Aunt Mary kept the cool cloths fresh on his forehead while Uncle Arley did his part, pacing the floor at the foot of the bed. Tam sat nearby, her eyes burning and red-rimmed from the day's exhaustion, but she knew sleep was beyond her.

A touch on the shoulder edged through the dullness she felt. She looked up to Grandpa's wan smile.

"No need to stay in here all night," he said.

In a daze Tam followed Grandpa out to the porch, to the cool night air. She swayed in the darkness and had to steady herself with a hand on the post.

"You all right?" Grandpa asked.

"I'm fine." She looked toward the barn. "Where'd Bray get to?"

"Don't know. I don't remember seeing him since the calving."

Tam thought back through the day, to the vague memories of the afternoon's events. They had become all tumbled up into a series of confused images. But one memory stood out in her tired mind. When she and Grandpa left the barn to look for Arley and the doctor, Bray had hung back. As Tam walked out into the failing afternoon, she had turned to call to the boy, but her cry died on her lips. Bray had gathered up the stillborn calf in his arms. And on his face was an unexpected smile of relief.

Tears started up in Tam's eyes all over again. "Grand-pa," she sobbed.

The old man wrapped her up in his arms. "There, there," he whispered as he stroked her hair.

"But Grandpa. I hurt Deb—his feelings. I didn't understand—"

"Hush, girl. Now you do. And when he wakes you can tell him."

Tam drew her head back and peered into Grandpa's face. "But he may not wake up. Grandpa, he may not." She buried her head into his shoulder and shook with uncontrollable sobs.

Grandpa cleared his throat, cleaning out the rattle of his own feelings. "Tam, we mustn't give up hope. Misery comes upon us soon enough without having to drag it in through the door."

"But all I did was hope. I didn't understand. If I would have known—"

"If you'da known," a voice interrupted them from down in the yard. "And if the moon was brass and all the little wee ones danced with shoes of glass." Bray Skoolle stepped out of the darkness and walked toward them. He leaned against the porch and stared into the night sky.

"Looky there." He nodded. "The moon's begun to ebb away. Soon she'll be gone. But back again, I'd say."

"Oh, Bray, don't make light," Tam said, wiping the tears from her cheeks. "We're worried sore."

Grandpa patted her shoulder. "It's all right. Let the boy be."

Bray glanced up at Tam and Grandpa. He laughed. "You needn't let the boy be. He'll be, whether you will or no."

His jovial rudeness confused Tam. The seriousness she had seen in his face throughout the day was gone, his puckish air returned and his voice high and lilting as before.

"Well, I'm off away," he said.

"Where are you going?" Tam asked.

"To look for something lost." Bray spun about and struck out toward the orchard. He disappeared in the shadows of the trees.

"Should I go after him?" Tam asked.

Grandpa shook his head.

"He's a trifle unfeeling, isn't he?" Tam said.

"I don't believe he's a bit of it."

A while later, Grandpa went in, complaining of an ache in his bones, and left Tam to the stillness of the night air. She was not ready just yet to return to Deb's bedside and to the waiting, so she stayed out on the porch and hugged her arms to herself, trying to calm the unease in her heart.

She gazed off toward the orchard and wondered if Bray had gone far. She wondered how he imagined he could find anything in the dark. Despite her unaccustomed fear, curiosity finally got the better of her. She stepped down into the yard and hurried to the gnarled tree under which she had last seen the boy.

It was difficult for the moonlight to find its way through the orchard's overhanging branches and boughs, so the darkness was near complete through the long rows of trees. Within that shadow, the evening air was no longer still. There was a rustling as faint breezes passed through the leaves to stir them up with constant whisperings.

Tam swallowed down the urge to run back to the house. She stepped under the dark canopy and followed after Bray, weaving her way through the trees. As she moved deeper into the orchard, however, her curiosity turned to worry. The boy was nowhere to be seen.

She stopped. A shiver rushed through her insides. Turning back, she sought the comfort of light from the house, but it was hidden from view.

"Bray," she called, near to panic. "Bray, where are you?"

There was no answer. She cast about trying to find the path back, but in the darkness her choices had become doubtful.

"Bray!"

With shadows nipping at her, she hurried on. She spied an open space ahead and felt a slight comfort of recognition. It was the clearing where Grandpa burned his prunings.

Light from the three-quarter moon shone upon a stack of wood in the middle of the open space—a pile built up of branches and split logs, arranged as if for a bonfire. A rustle of footsteps from off to the right made Tam's heart jump a beat. She shrank back behind the bole of an apple tree and searched through the shadows. Bray emerged into the clearing with a bundle cradled in his arms. He approached the pile and set his burden there.

Tam caught her breath. Bray had laid the dead calf on the stack of wood. He pulled an object out of the pocket of his overalls and knelt down. Sparks flew as he struck fire from his hand. Then with his face nearly down to the ground, he breathed a red and yellow life into the tinder. He fed kindling onto the new fire, coaxing it up into the wood. And then he stepped back. His body turned to a wavering silhouette as the flames licked up through the pyre.

Tam watched from the shadows. She was fascinated by the care Bray seemed to be taking for even the most disagreeable tasks of the farm. Uncle Arley would not have to worry now about disposing of the carcass.

But then Bray did a strange thing. With a slow lope he circled the growing blaze, jogging around and disappearing behind the fire, only to reappear on its other side. Tam watched bewildered as the boy turned from shadow to light with each circuit of the flames. And with each lap he ran faster, stirring up the dust of the clearing. Tam was about to call out to him, to ask what on earth he was doing, but he disappeared once more behind the blaze. A shower of sparks rose up from the bonfire, and though Tam waited expectantly he never reappeared on the other side.

Chapter Eighteen

THE NEXT MORNING brought no change to Deb. He lay pale and still on the bed, his breathing rapid and thin. Aunt Mary had tried to spoon a light broth between his lips, but it dribbled down his chin. She wiped it away with a towel and set the bowl of warm soup on the stand by the bed.

"I'll try again later," she said with a sigh. She turned to Tam. "Did you sleep at all?"

"Some." But Tam wasn't sure whether that was quite the truth. She had tossed and turned in bed, and might have dozed, but she wasn't convinced that counted. "Bray's gone." She plucked at her apron, smoothing it out over her knees.

"Oh?"

"Last night."

"Where'd he go?"

"Don't know. He just went away. But he took care of the calf before he left."

"He's been a good helper around here." Aunt Mary stood up from her chair and arched her back to stretch out the night's watching. "Ohhh, this is worrisome work."

"Maybe you should get some rest," Tam said.

"I'll be fine. There's too much to do to be resting now. Maybe later."

"When's the doctor coming back?"

"Sometime this morning. Though I'm afraid there's not much he can do right now."

"Oh." Tam had tried to convince herself that once Doc Williams returned everything would be all right, that he would bring a medicine or cure that would rouse Deb out of his deep slumber. "Isn't he rested enough? Shouldn't he be waking up now?"

Aunt Mary put her hand on Tam's shoulder. "Dear, he's not asleep."

Tam nodded. "I know. But looking at him, it seems like he's just napping and bound to wake at any time."

Aunt Mary gazed at Deb. Tam could see the gleam of tears forming in her eyes.

"Like he was asleep," her aunt whispered.

Tam left the room just as Uncle Arley came into the house. Lydia had a breakfast for him, ready warm on the table. But he passed it by and went on into the bedroom to check on Deb.

Tam wandered out of the house and across the yard. "Drat Deb," she said. "He should have just stayed put where he was. And drat Bray. Why'd he have to leave?"

Her grumbling took her past the barn and toward the creek. The morning sun, sparkling on the water's cheerful tumble, made an awkward discomfort well up inside her, so she sought refuge within the shade of the orchard. After wandering for a bit through the trees, she found herself back in the clearing. The bonfire of the night before had burned itself out, leaving only gray ashes where once there had been a great pile of wood and kindling.

Tam crossed to the spot. She remembered the roaring flames that had taken the calf. The night before, when she left the darkness under the trees to call out for Bray, the heat from the blaze had been intense, sending her back to the edge of the firelit clearing.

But now the light of morning shone about her as she kicked through the ashes. It seemed that everything had been burned to dust. Or almost everything. She bent to the ground. There, poking up through the ashes was a pile of sticks and twigs, arranged in a haphazard stack, untouched by any flame, just as Bray had set them two days ago.

She pulled a twig from the pile. At last, her pent-up emotion overflowed. "Deb," she sobbed, "please come back."

Chapter Nineteen

ONCE AGAIN, Deb struggled with shadows that pulled him between dreams and waking. Once again, an evil voice wove in and out of his consciousness.

"So you've come back," it said.

Deb struggled against its hold.

"I'll have you now," it said.

From a distance came another voice that sounded as if it rolled through water. "Hey, there! Get away! Pa, help me chase him away."

The first voice let out an angry cry that faded into the darkness. The second drew close, becoming more distinct.

"Pa, what do you think? A boy lying out here in nothing but his nightshirt."

"Is that so?" answered a third voice. "Where's his folk?"

"Don't know. The house don't seem nothing but empty. Barn, too. Seems we happened along just in time. The circle ain't been closed yet."

Deb opened his eyes to the voices. A blond-headed boy stood over him, his silhouette blurred hazy from the morning sun at his back.

Deb tried to block out the brightness with his hand.

"Who . . . who are you?" he asked.

"I'm Nate. My pa is Mr. Brookmire. Who are you?"

"Deb—er—Jacob. Jacob Corey." He sat up and looked about. He was in his own yard, near the stairs to his own house.

"Pa, you think he's addled?" Nate asked.

"It happens sometimes."

Deb jumped up and brushed the dirt from his night-shirt. He shook his head, trying to remember how he ended up in the front yard wearing hardly nothing. And standing on both legs. It all seemed a touch out of kilter, but he couldn't say why.

"Ma-a-a," Deb called toward the house. He started up the steps. "Ma, where are you?"

He pushed through the door. "Ma, you in here?" The great room stood quiet. Not even the creaking of the old clock answered back. It had stopped cold, with both hands pointing nearly straight up, not more than an hour past midday.

"Who you looking for?" Nate had followed him into the house.

Deb swung open the door to his parents' bedroom. It was empty. Not only were his folks gone, but all the furnishings Deb had become accustomed to were missing, too. No brass bed. No bedside table. Not even the armoire Ma had brought along when she married Pa.

"They in here?" Nate asked, thrusting his head through the door. "The people you're looking for? Are they here?"

Deb hurried upstairs to the loft, bounding up three steps at a time. "Ma? Where are you?"

His bed was gone, too. His clothes. All he ever knew in the world. He scrambled back downstairs.

"A fine house," Nate said. "Whose is it?"

Deb burst out the front door, leapt over the incomplete circle that had been traced in the earth near the foot of the steps, and raced toward the field. He shooed away the hawk perched on the fence and climbed up to get a better view.

"Pa-a-a-a!"

The field was laid with a green carpet of new hay. There was no sign that Pa had ever been in the middle of plowing for corn.

Deb hurried to the barn and pushed the door wide.

Not even the sound of a pigeon greeted him. Hilde was gone, her stall clean, the manger empty as if it were still waiting to be used.

"Grandpa! You in here? Where is everybody?"

"Maybe they've left," Nate said, still following. "Or they ain't here yet."

Deb raced back through the house again, checking every room. But it had been cleaned out, emptied of all the odds and ends that had built the place up into something livable. Everything was gone but for the clock on the mantel. And that was broke. Deb grabbed hold of the mantel, feeling like he was about to collapse on the floor. He breathed deep to steady himself.

After a bit, with his thoughts still all crumpled up with confusion, he staggered out to sit on the porch steps, just to get out of that empty house.

"What's happened?" he said, slumping down. "Where is everything?"

Nate sat beside him. "Don't you know?"

"No. Do you?"

"Course not. I wasn't here. Pa, Jacob Corey wants to know what happened."

Mr. Brookmire stood on the poplar-shaded road, holding the bridle of a small pony that was attached to a cart. He gazed off into the distance. "That's only natural," he said. "To want to know."

Deb buried his face in his hands, wishing he could steady the spinning of his head. "I don't understand. Why would my family leave like this without telling me?"

"Maybe they didn't leave you," Nate said. "Maybe you—"

But Deb didn't let him finish. He jumped down from the steps and snatched something from the grass near the half circle that had been drawn in the dirt. Something he recognized.

"Grandpa's silver penny!" He held the coin for Nate to see. "He gave it to me for luck after I broke my . . ." Deb's voice trailed off.

"Broke your what?" Nate asked.

Deb looked down at his leg. He stamped his foot on the grass.

"My leg," he said. He stamped again.

"Appears it got better," Nate said.

Deb held the penny in the palm of his hand. "I don't see how."

"Son," called Mr. Brookmire, "we ought to be heading on. We don't want moss growing under our feet."

"Yes, Pa. But what about this boy? We gonna just leave him here without his folks?"

"Don't know what else we can do, unless he wants to tag along with us. But you best get him a pair of pants."

Nate looked at Deb. "You wanna pair of pants?"

"No! I've gotta wait here for Ma and Pa. And Grandpa. And Tam. They'll be back. I'm sure they will."

"All right, I reckon." Nate turned and shambled across the yard to the road. Mr. Brookmire flicked the reins, and with a jingle, the pony yanked its cart into motion.

Deb sat back on the porch and ran a hand down his leg. The skin was smooth and unbroken, the bone beneath, firm and strong. Had he dreamt it all? Or had he returned again to his fever dreams?

No, this didn't have the feel of a dream about it. But neither did he feel completely awake. The vacant house at his back sent a chill down his spine. He glanced at the blank windows, at the door that led to nowhere familiar. The silence of the house crept out and around him, like it was trying to take hold and pull him in.

"Wait," he hollered. He jumped up and chased after Nate and Mr. Brookmire. "Wait for me."

"Maybe your folks come along this way," Nate said. "Either this way or t'other. This is the way we're going. Heading to home ourselves."

"To home?" Deb said.

"Yep," said Mr. Brookmire. "To home."

"We ain't been there in a long while," said Nate. "I wonder if it's changed much."

"No," said Mr. Brookmire, staring straight ahead, "it won't have changed. But if this boy's wandering about in just a nightshirt, hadn't *he* ought to change? Are you sure you wouldn't like a pair of pants?"

"Yeh, you ought to," Nate said. "Mine'd be too short in the leg and a tad narrow in the beam, but we can turn up a pair of Pa's for you."

Deb peeked down at his dusty feet and legs. "All right. Until we catch up to my folks."

Mr. Brookmire pulled at the pony's bridle. With a shake of its head, it clopped to a stop.

Nate hurried to the back of the cart. "A pair of yours, Pa?"

Mr. Brookmire nodded, still with his eyes on the road before them.

After a moment's rummaging, Nate returned with a pair of pants and a shirt.

"And a sack for your tack," he said, handing over a cloth bag.

Deb dropped Grandpa's silver penny into the bag, then removed the nightshirt and stuffed it in as well. He pulled on Mr. Brookmire's pants. They were a bit long, but Nate knelt down and turned up the bottoms into twice-folded cuffs.

"These'll do, Pa," Nate said.

Deb buttoned up the shirt, pushed its long tail into the pants, and pulled the suspenders over his shoulders.

"Sorry I ain't got no boots to borrow you," Nate said. "I'd give you mine, but your feet are a sight bigger."

Deb slung the sack over his shoulder. "I'll be fine."

"Well, let's be off then," Mr. Brookmire said. He shook the reins again, and the pony lurched forward into the morning.

While he walked alongside Nate, Deb looked about, searching for any sign that his Ma and Pa had passed this way. He shook his head more than once. He just couldn't figure out why they would have left without him. And why he couldn't remember how he came to be lying in the yard. And why his leg was healed all straight after what the doc had said. And where was Tam? Hadn't she come to visit?

Deb tried to grasp it all in his head, but hard thinking seemed to be just out of his reach.

"You okay?" Nate asked.

Deb nodded. He couldn't figure how to explain if he'd said no, but he felt like he had to say something more. "Where are we going?"

"Home," Nate said.

"Where's home?"

"Away off in the east, Pa says."

"Out to Winfield?" Deb asked. "My sister and her husband live there."

"Winfield?" asked Mr. Brookmire. "Where's that?"

"Well, if we keep on this road, we'll pass smack through it. Maybe that's where my folks are, with my uncle Andy."

"Then we'll just have to keep on this road," Mr. Brookmire said.

After a while, though Deb wouldn't say anything about it, his stomach began to rattle up against his insides with hunger. He couldn't remember the last time he'd eaten. It could've been days ago, for all he knew. And he was thirsty, too. At last his stomach growled its complaint aloud.

Nate glanced at the sun overhead. "I'm hungry, too," he said. "Pa, it's about time we took a break for some dinner, ain't it?"

Mr. Brookmire pulled the pony to a stop. "If you reckon. Why don't you get me my things before you start fixing the vittles."

"Yes, Pa." Nate hurried to the back of the cart and hauled out a canvas bag. He led Mr. Brookmire to a boulder that stuck up from the ground at the side of the road.

"What can I do to help?" Deb asked. His stomach was nagging at him to speed things along.

"I'll get a fire going," Nate said. "You fetch the fry-pan and the grub-sack from the cart there. They'll be wrapped up in my ma's star quilt."

Deb found the quilt and had everything unrolled quick as he could. By the time he carried it all to the side of the road, Nate had a fire going. Mr. Brookmire was settled on the rock, whittling at a block of wood with a short knife.

Nate took the frying pan and the food sack and soon had white beans and salt pork simmering over the flames. He mixed up a batch of cornmeal flour with a bit of sugar and water, then he spooned the batter onto the coals to cook up ash cakes.

"Smells good," Deb said. His stomach rumbled in agreement.

Mr. Brookmire looked up from his carving and focused on the air just over Deb's shoulder. "Sure does. Nothing like fresh air and sunshine to conjure up an appetite. The only hex that's sure." He turned back to his chunk of wood.

It was then that Deb paid attention to what Mr. Brookmire was doing. He was feeling the wood with his fingers, like he wasn't even seeing the work. His eyes seemed to wander about, glancing up and around and all about while he flicked at the block with the sharp knife, shaving off bits to uncover what his fingers had sensed in the wood.

"Nate," Deb whispered, "your pa carves by feel?"

"Oh, he has to," Nate said. "He can't see. He's blind as a bat."

Chapter Twenty

ONCE DINNER was ready and dished onto plates, Deb shoveled the steaming beans into his mouth like he'd never tasted anything so good. Mr. Brookmire was right about fresh air and sunshine being such a sure hex. Deb filled his plate twice and then sopped it all up with a couple of ash cakes.

"You ain't eaten in a while, have you?" Nate said, wiping his mouth with the back of his hand.

Deb shook his head. "I can't remember when."

"Well, we ought to finish up and be moving on," Mr. Brookmire said. "We don't want to be caught too long in one place."

"No, Pa. We'll get cleaned up."

Soon the boys had everything stowed back in the small wagon, wrapped up in Mrs. Brookmire's star quilt.

"Where is your ma?" Deb asked as they headed back onto the road.

"She didn't come with us," Nate said. "She'll likely follow later."

They continued on, and Deb continued wondering where *his* family had gotten to.

As evening crept into the sky, they made camp on the lee side of a small hill, up away from the road. Far off in the west, dark billowed clouds glimmered with lightning flashes. Deb could smell rain in the air.

"Pa," Nate said, "looks like a storm coming in."

"Best set up the shelter, then. First, pull out my things."

Once Mr. Brookmire was settled on the sloping hill, bent over his carving, Nate pulled an oilcloth from the wagon. Deb helped him tie it to the side of the cart, and together they stretched it out to form a lean-to anchored to the ground with stones.

"There, that'll do," Nate said. "Would take an almighty blast now to shake 'er loose."

Though supper that evening was a duplicate of the meal at midday, Deb savored it just the same. After they'd eaten and put everything away, the wind began to liven up. The canvas of their shelter flapped and popped in its stiff breeze.

"Storm for sure," Nate said.

Mr. Brookmire sniffed the moving air. "Feels like it." Then he held his carving toward the boys. "Look here. It's done."

Nate took it from his father. "It's real good." He handed it to Deb.

It was a galloping horse, alive with its mane streaming behind and its ears laid back and its hooves flashing with the speed of its flight.

A rumble of thunder rolled over the hills. Wind tugged through Deb's hair, pushing it into his face. He looked up. The sun had settled behind the advancing clouds.

"It's wonderful," he said, handing the carving back to Mr. Brookmire. "It looks like Betsy."

"Betsy?" Nate said.

"When she was younger."

Darkness grew about the small camp. The wind died and left in its wake an eerie calm. No moon or stars appeared in the sky overhead. The cloud ceiling was complete.

"Son," Mr. Brookmire said, "lead me to my bedding. I'm tuckered out."

"Yes, Pa."

Deb was tired, too. By the light of a single lantern, they all settled themselves within the shelter of the lean-to, secure from the threatening weather.

"G'night, Pa," Nate said. With a puff of breath, he blew out the lantern.

"Good night, son. And good night, Jacob Corey."

Deb lay back under a borrowed blanket, still in his borrowed pants and shirt, and still picking in his mind at the where and why and when of what had happened.

"Call me Deb," he said with a yawn.

In the middle of the night a single crack of thunder jerked Deb awake. Answering echoes rumbled from all around. Deb sat up and pulled his blanket about his shoulders. Splatters of rain plunked against the canvas of the shelter. The wind whipped against the oilcloth, making it billow and snap above them.

The pony whimpered.

Another flash of lightning lit the space beneath the lean-to. Thunder split the air. The pony cried out, her neighing fraught with panic.

"I'll see to her," Nate said, his sleepy face whitened by yet another flash.

"Try to calm her," Mr. Brookmire yelled over the thunder's roar. "She doesn't like the noise."

"Yes, Pa." Nate scooted out into the rain that now rattled the canvas above them.

Another flash lit up the night, followed by another cracking of the sky. The pony neighed again.

"Whoa," Nate cried out. "Whoa! Now get back here. Oh, c'mon . . ." His voice trailed off into the storm.

Deb scrambled from under the shelter. Through the brilliance of the lightning he could see Nate chasing up the hillside after the frightened pony. Deb raced to help head her off.

It became a wild chase, trying to catch the poor pony between the cracks of thunder that spooked her farther into the night. The boys called to each other over the gale, shouting out instructions.

"Over there, cut her off."

"She's thisaway."

"Head her up the hill."

"Look out, she's a-comin' down."

They finally hemmed her in within a low valley. Nate eased toward her. "Whoa, girl," he said. "It's all right. Steady."

Though the rain continued unabated, the thunder had rumbled off into the distance. The wind slackened, giving them a chance to get close enough for Nate to stroke a soothing hand across the pony's flank.

"There you go," he whispered. "Pretty soon you'll be right as rain." And then he looked into the dark sky and laughed. "Right as rain! Lawd, that's a joke."

Deb laughed, too, standing soaked to the skin, his backside muddied from slipping and sliding down the slope of a hill.

"We best get back," he said with a grin, "before we get all wet ourselves!"

"Yep, before we wash clean away."

Together they led the pony across the rolling hills. By the time they got within sight of their camp, the storm had moved on, turning its fury to the distances. A misty moon managed to peek through tattered clouds.

"Pa!" Nate broke into a run, leaving Deb and the pony behind. "Pa!"

"Nate, what's wrong?" Deb tugged on the pony's bridle, pulling her after him.

Nate reached the camp. The canvas of their makeshift shelter flapped in the breeze that followed the storm. The gale had torn the oilcloth from its anchor. All their belongings were drenched.

Nate searched frantically through the campsite.

"What is it?" Deb asked.

"Pa's gone." The boy's face was stricken with a pale distress. "He's gone."

Chapter Twenty-one

P_{A}, WHERE ARE YOU?" Nate called out at the top of his voice.

Deb followed him back into the night. "Let's get the lantern," he said. "Maybe he'll see the light."

"No, he won't. He *can't* see." Nate ran ahead. "Pa! Are you there?"

There was no answer.

He turned and raced back past Deb. "He could've gone anywheres. Maybe the way we come." He ran through camp and down to the road, almost losing his footing on the wet slope. Deb kept close behind. He felt foolish for his suggestion to use the lantern, but there was a helpless fluttering in the pit of his stomach that he thought he could drive out with action.

"Maybe he followed the road," Deb said.

"He's blind. He can't tell the road from nothing. He could be anywheres."

"Well, we can't just go running helter-skelter."

Nate glanced both ways along the muddy trail. "What if he's hurt?" he said. "Or struck by lightnin'? Or blowed away by the storm? Or. . . . What'll I do?"

"We'll find him. He's got to be somewhere. Maybe by daylight—"

"We gotta find him now," Nate said. "He'll get caught if we don't find him."

"Caught? By what?"

"We *gotta* find him!"

"Then let's do it smart. He must have left a trail. We just need to follow it."

"Naw, that's no good." Nate shook his head. "The storm's washed away his tracks. There's nothing but mud."

"All right, then, let's circle out from the camp. We can cover a lot of ground—and maybe not miss him in the dark."

Nate sucked in a shuddering breath and nodded his head. "I'll get the pony." He scurried back to camp.

By the time the eastern sky had flushed to pale yellow, the boys' voices were hoarse from calling over the empty hills. Deb nodded in exhaustion. He clutched his arms about Nate's waist to keep from sliding off the pony. Their senses had been stretched taut for half the night. Time and again their hopes had risen, only to be dashed away. They saw Mr. Brookmire's shirt in each pale outcropping of rock. Each starlit glimmer of standing water belied his movement across the grass. They were worn out from the disappointments.

But for an occasional snuffling shiver, Nate rode quiet. He let the pony wander where she would. Both boys were cold from the wet of the night before, but their huddling brought no comfort.

"We should rest," Deb said. "Make a fire."

"No," Nate mumbled. "Must find Pa."

"We could get back to camp. Get warm and eat. Then come back to here and start over."

The pony shambled to a stop. Deb slid off her back and turned to help Nate down.

Nate's face was streaked with tears. "Where could he be?" He sank to the ground. "There's nowheres else. We've looked everywheres. He must be caught."

"It's awful wet here," Deb said. "We should go back and get dry."

"I'm gonna keep lookin'!"

"All right, all right. It was just an idea." Deb peered toward the east. He shivered. "The sun is coming up. Maybe it'll warm us a bit."

Though the hills about them were still awash with the blue light of early morning, a blush of rose had begun to seep through the mists. Deb walked to the edge of shadow and stepped into the full light of morning. Its warmth felt fine on his face.

But then he caught a movement out of the corner of his eye. Upon a rise of earth just to his left, he saw a ragged old man stooped over another on the ground.

"Hey!" Deb called. "What are you doing there?"

Nate pushed past him and chased toward the two men. "Pa!"

With a growl, the old man swept away to disappear around the hillside. Deb hurried to catch up to Nate. Lying on the ground was Mr. Brookmire.

Nate shook him. "Pa, wake up."

Mr. Brookmire groaned. Nate shook him again. "He almost got you. Jacob Corey found you just in time."

Mr. Brookmire rolled to his back. "Son, is that you?"

"Yes, Pa."

"Where have you been?" He struggled to sitting. "I've been worried near ill." He clutched his son's shoulders and held on tight. "I was afraid you'd been blowed away by the storm. You took so long. Didn't you hear me calling?"

"No, Pa. We thought *you* was blowed away—or struck by lightnin'. Didn't figure you'd be out lookin' for us."

"Wasn't exactly *lookin'*," Mr. Brookmire said. "But I couldn't just sit about thinkin' you boys was lost."

"I know, Pa."

Deb climbed up the short slope. "It's lucky you didn't go farther," he said. "It's a straight fall onto rocks down there."

Nate helped Mr. Brookmire to his feet and led him to where Deb stood. "Yes, Pa. It's plain—" He stopped and stared into the distance, his face flushing with excitement.

"Plain what?" Mr. Brookmire asked.

"Pa," Nate said, "we're home. Away down there. Home."

Deb followed Nate's pointing hand. The mists parted to reveal a view filled up with morning light—a valley of well-ordered fields, dotted here and there with houses and barns that glimmered in the new sunshine. Scattered ponds reflected the blue of the sky. And in the distance, near the bending of the earth, the spires of a city pierced the clouds.

"Home?" Mr. Brookmire said. "Home at long last?"

"Yes, Pa. Don't it feel wonderful?"

Deb could feel it, too, though he couldn't have said exactly why. "That's not Winfield," he said. But still it felt like a place he wanted to be.

"Son," Mr. Brookmire said, "where's our gear?"

"Back to camp, where we left it."

"We must collect it all."

"Yes, Pa."

Mr. Brookmire rode the pony, with Nate leading the way. Deb followed close behind, though he couldn't help glancing back over his shoulder. His mind was more confused than ever. He was eager to go to that peaceful valley where everything was right, but he struggled with the feeling that going there wouldn't bring him any closer to finding Ma and Pa.

"I went farther than I thought," Mr. Brookmire said when they arrived at camp. "Worry makes for long nights, I reckon."

"Sure does, Pa." Nate helped his father down. "But daytime floods it right away."

"It does indeed. Even for a blind man like me. But let's not let the morning waste away."

Deb helped Nate pull up the oilcloth and shake off the last remaining beads of moisture. They rolled up the cloth and stowed it in the cart while Mr. Brookmire gathered the blankets and bedding.

"Collect your things, Jacob Corey," he said.

After a short search Deb found his bag snagged on a bush halfway up the hillside. The gale had turned it inside out, spilling its contents on the ground. Deb retrieved the damp nightshirt and stuffed it back into the sack. He was about to return to camp when his eye caught something shining in the grass. He picked up the object and carried it down the hill, weighing it in his hand.

"'Twas a mighty storm," Nate said. "Seems them clouds beats on this country like a drum. It'll be good for us all to get down to home, I reckon. Come on, Jacob Corey, gather up your gear."

Deb only stared at the silver piece.

"Hurry," Nate said. "Daylight's wastin'."

"I . . . I'm not going with you," Deb finally said.

"Why, sure you are. You'll be more than welcome."

"That's not my home." He continued to stare at the object in his hand. "It's nothing like where I come from." His eyes were dazzled by the sun's reflection off the silver. "I can't go to that place. I have a home."

"But there's nobody there," Nate insisted.

"There must be." Though he couldn't explain why, as he stared at the coin Deb felt certain he could find them.

"But—"

"Son," Mr. Brookmire said, "young Jacob knows his mind. Let him have a blanket and some food, and let's be on our way."

"Thank you," Deb said, "but I'll be fine." He shoved the coin into his bag.

"Nonsense. You'll need a blanket in case it storms again. And since you were so kind to help my boy last night"—he felt his way to the cart and pulled his burlap sack from its corner—"take this." He fished the horse carving from the bag. "Come, take it."

"You've given me so much already."

"Ah, but the only thing out of all this that is really mine to give are my little carvings." He held the horse out. "Please?"

Deb accepted the piece from Mr. Brookmire and placed it in his sack along with the silver penny.

Chapter Twenty-two

ON THE LONG WAY BACK toward his family's farm, Deb kept pulling out the silver penny and staring at it. Grandpa'd said it was good luck. Deb wondered how much the luck would hold. It did seem like the coin had broken that long-ago hex of the cure for wanderlust. Seemed he was free now to go wherever he chose. There just didn't seem to be anybody to leave behind or anywhere to get to.

Maybe the penny's luck would continue and allow him to find his folks. "Help me, please," he said, addressing the face on the coin. King George the Second simply stared on in silence.

Late in the day Deb still wasn't back to home. He must have traveled farther than he thought with Nate and Mr. Brookmire. But then he had been on the road with them most of yesterday and hadn't had a good start until nearly noon today. He was footsore and hungry and just plain wore out. He decided he ought to stop for the night. He settled himself at the side of the road, beneath a tree—an outlier of a wood that had pushed the road into a horseshoe bend. He ate a portion of the food Nate had given him: jerky and hard bread. He also found a water sack Nate had stowed in the bag. He took a long drink. Nate had been more than thoughtful.

With his head resting against the tree trunk, Deb looked about. The sun filtered through the woods behind him, dappling the ground with evening shadow and light. Now that he was still, the sleepless night and the long walk caught up with him, making his whole body slump with exhaustion.

He closed his eyes. A recollection crept through the fog that had formed in his head. He could almost feel the tree bark under his hand as, in memory, he climbed through spreading branches. He could almost smell the ripened fruit. Tam's voice called to him from below. "Your ma will skin you if you rip your pants."

He remembered laughing as he dropped her a perfect apple. "I'll just have to go bone-naked then."

Deb started awake at a snuffling, shuffling noise. Backed by a late morning light, a hunched and grubby figure hovered over him—a man with wild hair and a face twisted with age.

"I told you, you'd not escape me so easy," the man hissed.

It was the voice from his fever! With a gasp, Deb rolled away and jumped to his feet.

"Get back here," the man cried. "You can't cheat me."

Deb set himself to flee from the crazy-looking man, but he hesitated. The man stood over the bag that contained all Deb had in the world: his nightshirt and blanket, the food and water, Mr. Brookmire's carved horse, and the silver penny.

"Give me my bag," Deb said.

The man looked down. "Ahhh." He snatched up the bag. "Come and get it."

"It's mine!"

"You're mine, too. And long overdue. I'll not let you go this time."

"Give me my bag!"

"Well, let's just see what you've got in here." With a grimy hand, the old man pulled out the nightshirt. "You'll not be needing this." He dropped it to the ground. "Nor this," he said about the blanket. He stared at the horse carving for a moment, then dropped it, too.

He crumbled up the bread and scattered it about him. He took a drink from the water skin and tossed it away, with the water still dribbling down his chin.

"Now, what's this?" He pulled his hand out of the bag closed around something small. But then he shrieked and cast the thing away as if it had burned him.

Holding his hand, he jumped about on one foot, whimpering and moaning. "A confederacy of angels," he gasped. "I should have known."

Deb raced to retrieve the penny.

The old man backed away. "Your luck can't hold forever," he said. Then he turned and fled through the trees.

Deb squeezed the penny in his fist. "Yes, it can!"

Deb had been so tired he must have slept through the whole night and most of the morning. By the time the old man had awakened him, the sun was already creeping toward noon. After another long afternoon of walking, Deb's surroundings finally became more familiar. He turned a bend and spied the poplars that shaded the road leading to his home. He started to run, but then he stopped in caution. Someone was sitting on the front porch, as if waiting for him. At first Deb thought it might be the old man returned, but the thatch of red hair that shone in the evening sun showed otherwise.

Still, Deb approached with caution. "Who are you?" he called.

A boy looked up from whatever he was fiddling with.

Deb recognized him. "It's you. Where's Tam? Where's my family? I knew you were bad luck. You've driven them all away!"

The boy held up the clock from the mantel. "It's stopped," he said. "I thought I might fix it."

"It's not yours."

"Nah, it's not." He set the clock down next to him. "But still I thought I might try."

Deb climbed up to the porch and retrieved the old timepiece. He set it back inside, on the mantel where it belonged.

"Where's my family?" he called. "Where's everybody gone?"

"They ain't here yet," the boy said. He stood in the doorway. "But maybe I can help you find them."

"I don't need your help. Why don't you just go away? Nobody wants you here."

The smile dropped off the redheaded boy's face.

Deb pressed his advantage. "Why don't you just go find your own folk? Get off where you belong? I don't need you. I don't want you."

"Is that what you say?" the boy asked. "Is that what you want?"

"Yes! Just go away!"

The boy seemed to slump at Deb's words. He stared at Deb for the longest time. Deb shifted uncomfortably. "I meant what I said."

The boy turned and left the house. Deb felt a sudden dropping in his own heart. He hurried to the door, looking to call the boy back, but he was gone, vanished in the evening light that had already grown under the orchard trees.

Darkness descended like a blanket over the house. Deb couldn't bring himself to remain inside all alone, so he sought comfort beneath the trees. He wound his way along until he came to a clearing. He crossed to the middle and looked up at the sky. A deep blue arched overhead, sprinkled with the first few stars of night. The despair of loneliness filled his heart.

"Where is everyone?" he cried. Looking at the ground, he tried to stifle his anguished feelings in his hands. At his feet he saw a small pile of sticks, set there as if a' purpose. With a kick, he scattered them across the clearing.

He wouldn't return to the empty house, to its reminders, so he curled up in his blanket near the edge of the trees. For the longest time he lay awake staring at the stars until his eyes could no longer focus. At last he welcomed the forgetfulness of sleep.

A bone-wrenching yank jolted Deb awake, followed by a dizzying sensation as he was swept off the ground to dangle by his foot.

"I told you your luck wouldn't hold."

Deb's head jerked and bounced as he was carried along, hanging upside down. He could hardly make a sound. All he could do was flail his arms in vain.

"H-h-help!" he cried at last.

"There's no one to help you now."

He was dropped headfirst with a thud.

"Look about you."

It was the old man from yesterday. A gloat spread across his face. He grinned, showing yellowed and crooked teeth.

Deb tried to scramble back but something knocked him forward. He tried to roll away to the side but again something stopped him. He burst out toward the man but was knocked down to his backside. It wasn't anything he could feel, just something that pinioned him to that small spot of ground.

Deb cast about in desperation.

"I made it afore I caught you," the old man cackled. "And your cursed talisman can't save you now."

A ring had been drawn in the dirt, there in the middle of the clearing. Again Deb tried to scramble out of its bounds, but he was trapped. And his bag with the silver penny lay on the ground, back where he'd left it when he went to sleep the night before.

The old man danced about him with glee, bouncing from one foot to the other.

> *HEART A-CHURNING,*
> *SOUL A-BURNING*
> *LONGINGS THAT WILL NEVER BE.*
> *WHOSOEVER*
> *HELD FOREVER*
> NOTHING *NOW CAN SET YOU FREE.*

Chapter Twenty-three

THE LOFT WAS EMPTY but for Tam. Aunt Mary had made up the bed. The blankets were smoothed out and the pillow fluffed and propped against the headboard. True to her nature, Aunt Mary had set everything neat and ordered. The crutch that Bray carved from the apple branch lay at the foot of the bed, angled across the quilt.

Tam lifted it and tucked the padded support under her arm. With a hopping step, she tried it out, crossing the floor to the far window. There she stopped. Down below Grandpa was heading toward the barn with a plate of food.

"Bray's gone," Tam whispered. "It'll just go to waste."

Grandpa disappeared through the doors of the old building. Tam carried the crutch back to its place.

"It would've been just right for Deb," she said.

She climbed onto the bed herself and lay on her back with her arms at her sides. Morning shadows made the room feel soft. The sounds from outside became clearer— as if all the farmyard noises were trying to crowd themselves up into the loft.

"It's my fault," Tam said. "I know it is." She closed her eyes, but she didn't cry. Instead she tried to think of some way, if it were ever possible, that she could tell her cousin she was sorry for driving him away.

Chapter Twenty-four

G*OT HIM NOW,* got him good," the old man prattled to himself. "Had him once, almost twice. Third time is the greatest charm." He glared at Deb, slumped on the ground. "Told you that I'd make you mine."

Again Deb tried to push out of the circle, but he was held fast, like the toad he had captured all those ages ago.

"Let me go! I've got to go."

The man laughed again. "You don't got to do nothing no more. Just sit there and wait."

Deb thrashed about, but it was no use. He couldn't budge himself an inch out of that charmed ring.

The man wriggled with delight. "Just sit there and wait till time is gone and you fade away into nothing. Ha, *ha*. Now I'm off to catch some more."

He hopped and skipped toward the edge of the clearing, his antics belying his age. Though he disappeared through the trees, Deb could still hear his voice. "Another 'un that'll never walk about again."

Once more Deb thrust himself at the invisible wall that held him, only to fall sprawling to the ground.

The sun turned overhead, wheeling through the daylight hours and on into evening and night. Stars streaked across the sky. The moon rose and set in one sweeping movement. It was as if the whole world passed about him, while he was stuck, the center of it all yet unable to be a part of it.

He sank farther into himself. He'd had this dream before. This nightmare of imprisonment.

The apple trees blossomed, the fruit ripened, the leaves turned gold and fell to the ground. Shadows danced through the days and nights and days. Deb's fear grew from panic to misery to despair to hopelessness and, at long last, to a lethargic indifference.

Through the blur that was the world around him, a face floated into view, intruding on Deb's solitude.

"Now will you let me help?"

Deb shook his head slowly, trying to remember how to speak. "I . . . I can't get out."

"You can, but there must be a replacement." A boy stepped into the circle with Deb, crowding him to its very edge. The boy pushed. Deb floundered backward, tripping over his own feet. He fell hard to the dirt. Outside the circle.

"Now go!" the boy commanded. "Get away from here." He pointed toward the west. "To the mountains. You'll find the way. Follow the stream. Up into the hills. Through the mist. With luck, you'll find your folk, your home."

"But—"

"Please go. And don't get caught again, or all this will have been in vain."

Deb rattled his head, shaking it free from the circle's grip. The trees were unchanged, the sky calm and still.

"Go!" the boy insisted.

Deb jumped to his feet and ran to the edge of the clearing. He turned to see the red-haired boy slump to the ground in the circle. "Go," the boy repeated in a voice Deb could barely hear.

Deb snatched up his bag, so relieved to be free he felt like crying and laughing all at once. His mind couldn't decide which to do, so he simply turned and raced through the orchard. What had the boy said? Follow the stream?

Deb hurried to the creek and splashed through its water to the trail on the far side. Once on the smooth, easy cow path he ran full out. He ran until his heart hammered and his lungs burned. He ran until his legs turned weak and his side ached. He fled along the track until his chest near burst. At last he had to stop. He bent over with his hands on his knees, gasping for breath.

But he hadn't outrun the turmoil in his mind. Long ago he thought he had left this dreamlike place, this home that wasn't home, when he came out of his fevered dreams, when he woke that morning to Ma and the silver penny. Now he couldn't understand what had happened to him. He just couldn't seem to get outside himself to think what it all meant.

He looked about at the unfamiliar scene. Though parts of it reminded him of home, it wasn't the same. The path he was on ran through an unknown pasture. In the distance a horse grazed on the lush, green grass. Deb stared hard at the horse.

"Betsy!"

At long last, here was a familiar presence. He raced across the meadow.

"Betsy," he cried as he wrapped his arms about her neck. She smelled of horsehair and hay. Her coat was warm against his check. She pushed gently against him.

"Look," he said. He pulled out Mr. Brookmire's carving. "This is you. Running like that day we jumped the

fence. Running like you were young again and I was—
Before we were— Before you . . ."

Understanding dropped into his heart like a stone.
"Am I . . . ?" But he couldn't bring himself to say it. He
sank to the ground. Betsy nickered as if to say, "It's all
right, I'm here," but her presence brought no comfort
at all.

Chapter Twenty-five

TAM PEEKED into Aunt Mary's room. Deb lay on the bed, quiet and still. He hadn't moved since last she looked in. In fact he hadn't stirred since Uncle Arley carried him there three days ago. She tiptoed into the room in her stocking feet.

Grandpa sat in the corner with his head in his hands.

"Hello, Grandpa," Tam whispered.

He looked up. "Morning, sweet 'un. Where's your aunt?"

"Resting, finally. She took to Lydia's bed."

"That's good. She's been mighty tuckered. Eh, now, where's your shoes?"

"I left them off. Aunt Mary doesn't need me clomping around, making all that racket. But if I thought it would wake up Deb, I'd wear horseshoes and jump and stomp all over the place."

Grandpa chuckled. "There's not much we wouldn't do for that. But I'm afraid all we can do is wait."

"And hope, Grandpa?"

"Yep. And that." He stood up. "Darlin', I need to stretch a bit. Would you mind watching?"

"No, Grandpa. I don't mind."

After he left the room, Tam pulled the chair near to the bed and sat, leaning close so she could look into Deb's face. His breathing continued faint. His skin was pale, his body still. She brushed a strand of hair off his forehead. Beads of sweat dampened his upper lip. With her sleeve she blotted the moisture away. She leaned closer still, near down to his ear, and whispered, "Deb, please come back."

Chapter Twenty-six

*H*AD DEB DREAMED the words? It was only a tiny voice from far away. "Please come back," it said. Come back? How could he? He might just as well be caught in that circle in the middle of Grandpa's clearing.

He opened his eyes to a misty daylight. Through the tattered branches of the tree overhead, Deb could see the gray dome of cloud that had hidden the sky.

He'd left Betsy behind. He'd left behind that reminder of what must be true. Once, he and Tam had come across the carcass of a deer lying in the creek. Curiosity had drawn them close, but finding that the deer was long dead drove them back away. Betsy reminded him of that deer. He had to get away from her.

He was on his way to find Nate and Mr. Brookmire.

They had offered him a place with them, down in that peaceful valley amongst the pleasant fields and farms. Or maybe in the city, with its gleaming spires. A place as much like heaven as Deb could imagine. No wonder it had tugged at him so. Perhaps it was where he belonged. If he'd understood, he would have gone with them then and there.

But now he was lost. He knew the tranquil valley lay to the east, but he had yet to get to somewhere familiar that would lead him there. To further his frustration, a wide forest lay directly in his path. And he was thirsty and hungry. He'd eaten the last crumbs that remained in his bag. He had made up his mind, however, and would continue east, straight through those dark woods. After all, what worse thing could happen to him?

He hitched his bag up on his shoulder and set out into the forest gloom. With the cloud cover overhead and the overarching trees, a deep twilight held sway within the woods. Dense undergrowth made progress slow.

Deb crept through the tangled brush. In the distance he heard a rushing noise that whispered between the earth and the canopy of leaves—like the sound of wind in the treetops. He pushed forward, crawling over rotted logs and through twisted vines. At a small opening in

the trees, he peeked up at the sky. A glimmer of lightning silhouetted the leaves and branches for an instant,
then the sky turned gray again.

He hurried on. The rustling sound became clear. It
was the splashing and chattering of a brook. He pushed
his way through a mess of chokecherry bushes and
almost tumbled into the pool that rippled at his feet.
Across the water, the creek plunged over a ledge of
mossy rocks into the deep pool.

The water reminded him of his thirst. He knelt and
scooped up a handful. It tasted of moss and forest rain.
He reached for another but stopped with his hand in the
air. Something was looking at him. He could feel it. He
scanned the woods. There was nothing there, but still
his hair prickled up on the back of his neck. He
crouched behind the ferns that overflowed the bank.

It was difficult to pierce the gloom, but at the very
edge of sight he caught a movement. Across the pool,
up on the far ledge where the creek babbled out of the
forest, a beaked head swiveled about to stare at him. Deb
stood, and the bird rose up, spreading its wings. It cried
out a piercing screech and sprang from its perch, only to
be jerked back down in a tangle of feathers. It lurched to
its feet, shook out its wings, and folded them up to its
side.

It was a hawk.

Once more it tried to rise in flight but again was yanked out of the air.

Must be caught up on something, Deb thought. He skirted the near side of the pool to get a closer look. The bird jerked its head about to follow him.

At the waterfall's edge Deb hesitated for just a moment. Then he climbed across the creek. The cold water splashed his legs and arms. He slipped, soaking his clothes in the icy stream. The bird arched its wings and opened its beak with a soundless threat.

"Easy, you." Deb wiped his cheek with the back of his hand. "I can help."

The bird staggered sideways and blinked its eyes in the forest twilight.

"It's all right." Deb pulled himself up to the rocky ledge.

With a powerful flapping of wings, the hawk tried to take flight once more. Deb could feel the wind of it on his face.

"Whoa. You'll just make it worse. I reckon you're all tangled up on something." He kept wary of the sharp beak and curved talons that clutched at the underbrush. "Easy. Easy, now."

He reached up toward the tangle that had trapped the bird.

"Ouch!"

Deb snatched back his hand and stuck it in his mouth to suck the painful bite.

"I'm only trying to help." He reached up with the other hand, his eyes fixed on the hawk. He was quicker this time and avoided the stabbing beak.

"All right. If you care to be that ill-mannered, I'll just let you be."

He eased himself down the rocks and across the falls. He shook his head at the stubborn bird. "You can just stay put."

A drop of water made him blink. He glanced up through the trees. Another drop splashed on his cheek. Glimmering circles flitted across the surface of the pool. Then the shower began in earnest. The hawk hunched itself up against the rain, clutching and bobbing on its haphazard perch.

"Dratted bird!" Deb yelled. "If you'd a' let me help, you wouldn't be stuck in that mess."

The rush of the storm through the trees drowned out the noise of the brook. Deb sought shelter under a dripping maple while the rain gusted up sheets across the pool. The waterfall thrashed at its banks and turned muddy and wild. With a frantic flapping of wings and a wild screech, the hawk shook and pulled against its binding.

Deb could see its peril.

"Dratted bird!" Deb turned and pushed his way through the ferns once more. His shirt clung to his back with the wet.

The muddy water tugged at his feet. He slipped on the stones and nearly tumbled into the current, but he was able to catch hold of the undergrowth and pull himself up to the ledge. The hawk screamed at him, wild with panic. It slashed at him with its beak. Deb pushed back with the flat of a hand and shoved the hawk into the brush. Talons tore at him. He heaved himself upward and pinned the bird down with his weight. Fumbling in the cold and wet, he found a leather strap tied about the hawk's leg. With difficulty he managed to loosen the strap from the hawk.

As Deb eased his weight off the bird, it thrust out its wings and knocked him off balance. Deb clutched at the tether that was still tangled in the brush. The hawk sprang up, jumping into the air with a flap of its wings.

For a moment Deb forgot the clawing pain in his hands and arms. He watched the soaring flight through the rain. With a graceful power, the hawk rose through the trees to disappear into darkness.

Deb felt a slight giving way at his feet, and then the bank on which he stood collapsed. He slid into the torrent, his hand still wrapped up in the leather strap. The cold of the water stopped his breath. He tried to pull himself up, but his weight and the pounding water tore the tether loose.

He flailed at the stream. He grasped at the slippery rocks. The swollen current churned through the pond. Deb was swept away from the near bank. He struggled to keep his head up. He slapped at the water with his hands and pushed with his legs, but he was no swimmer.

He thrust his chin out of the water. The rough current rolled him over. It knocked him about and pulled him downstream into darkness.

Chapter Twenty-seven

THE FIRST THING Deb became aware of was the passage of time. The next was the steady drone of rain upon a roof. And then he became conscious of the comfort wrapped all about him. From a deep sleep, he awoke to find himself buried in blankets, his head resting on a pillow. There was a ceiling overhead and the smell of damp wood and pine tar.

"Grandpa?"

He rose to his elbows, but the room was unfamiliar. And the man who sat next to the open hearth was a stranger. The man nodded toward Deb and then stood to stir up the fire.

"How's your arms feeling, then?" the man asked.

Deb looked at his arms, puzzled by the scratches that

raked his skin. Then he remembered the hawk. He gingerly touched the stinging gashes.

Gray light drizzled through rain-streaked windows. The room had the look and feel of a small cabin: four log walls, a single plank door set between two mullioned windows, and a rock fireplace. Stretched out on a rope before the hearth were a shirt, a nightshirt, a blanket, a pair of pants, and his bag. Deb realized he was naked. He pulled the bed coverings tight about him.

"Where's the rest of my things?"

The man pointed with his chin to a small table at the foot of the bed. Set out on its surface were a leather strap and a carving of a horse. Deb jumped up from the bed. He shivered in the damp air. "There was more."

"That's all there was." The man's deep voice resonated in the close space of the cabin. With a nod toward the makeshift clothesline, he continued, "But your bag's just about dry."

Deb yanked the bag off the line. He searched down inside.

"Everything else is hanging there," the man said.

Deb turned the bag inside out and shook it. He pulled at the seams. The cloth ripped a little. A small object dropped to the floor and rolled up against the man's booted foot.

"Well looky here," the man said. He picked up the

object. "I reckon it's not all there on the table after all. Look at this. A penny from George the Second! I haven't seen one of those since . . ." He squinched up his face in thought. " . . . why, since . . ." He dropped back to his chair and pushed a hand up through his hair. "Well, you know, I—I used to have one as a good-luck piece, but I loaned it away."

Deb thrust out his hand. "It's mine. Give it to me."

"All right, all right. Here you go." The man shook his head. "You ought to get yourself covered up. It's a bit damp today. You're all gooseflesh and shivers." He stood and felt the hanging pants. "These are about dry."

Deb grabbed his clothes off the line. The material was warm against his skin. He pulled on the pants and buttoned up the shirt.

"Now, what about something to eat?" the man asked. "I've a stew on the hob."

"No. I need to be getting on."

"Getting on? Just listen to them clouds pounding on the trees. You ought to stay here for a bit. Get some food in that belly. Some rest. Wait for a break in the weather. Then I'd be more than happy to help you on your way."

"I don't need any help." Deb shoved the penny into his pants pocket and gathered together the items on the table.

"Why, I reckon you do need some help. You need to eat. You need to rest. Or you'll just end up like I found you, facedown in the mud."

Deb spun about, dropping Mr. Brookmire's carving in his anger. "Who are you to tell me what I need?"

"Who am I? Well, I reckon we haven't been introduced, have we? My name is Jeremiah Turley. Now tell me who *you* are that you've no need of advice from those that care."

Deb stepped back, startled at the rebuke. And the name. After a brief hesitation, he ducked down to pick up the horse, but it had broken in two when it hit the floor. The man lifted one of the halves—the front part with its flowing mane.

"That's a shame," he said. "'Twas a pretty piece of work." He handed the piece to Deb.

Deb sat on the edge of the bed, struggling with disbelief. "Mr. Turley? You're Mr. Turley?"

"Why, boy, you say that as if you know of me."

Deb pulled the penny back out of his pocket. "I guess this isn't mine, after all."

Mr. Turley squinted in the dim light. "What's that?"

"The penny. It's not really mine. Only borrowed. I think it must be yours."

"Hmph. How could that be?"

"Well, it's not mine." Deb flipped the silver piece across the room. "Nothing's mine anymore."

"Boy—"

But Deb would not listen to another scolding. He was at the door, pulling it open before Mr. Turley could get another word out.

"I'll be on my way now," Deb said. He stepped out into the rain and banged the door closed behind him.

A path descended into a wooded ravine on the left. To the right, the trail climbed through the dripping trees. Before him was a steep fall into nothing. Deb took the upward path. The steady drizzle had brought a chalky stream of runoff that flowed along the trail. Rain streaked through Deb's hair and dribbled over his face. He wiped his eyes and continued on, but now that he was up and moving, he realized the truth of what Mr. Turley had said. His insides felt hollow with hunger, and there was a faintness lurking just behind his eyes. And with the wet came cold.

Deb stopped and looked back toward the cabin. A shiver took him, rattling through his shoulders. He wrapped his arms about himself and tried to control the trembling, but he was chilled through. He fought back tears of anger and frustration.

"I can do for myself!" he shouted. He stamped his

bare foot—and slipped. His feet flew out from under him before he could catch himself. He hurtled down the steep slope. He clutched at the undergrowth that whipped by. As he plunged over a ledge, he caught a tangle of roots in his hands. A shower of wet leaves and earth cascaded over him, pulled along by his slide through the brush. He sputtered and shook the debris out of his face. And then he let his heart give full rein to its hammering. Beneath his dangling feet was a long fall that disappeared into mist.

He feared to move. A shift of grip could cost him his hold altogether and send him plummeting to the depths below. He closed his eyes. An ache of tension ran through his arms and hands and fingers. It would be easy to let go. After all, what could be worse than death? Maybe there would at least be forgetting.

He looked back up the slope and took a last deep breath. But there, just beyond his reach, something glittered in the forest mold. Deb sobbed aloud, and his whole body shook. "Grandpa," he cried. And though his muscles were weak from hunger and fear, he pulled. He clinched his jaw and strained against the rebellion of his body and pulled again. With all the strength left to him, he pulled once more and was on the slope, scrambling to brace his feet against a leaning tree. There he rested, his breath in tatters, while the rain continued to fall.

Deb crawled back up the slope toward the trail, Grandpa's coin clutched in his hand. He kept to his hands and knees, wary of the slippery earth. At last he struggled onto the path and hauled himself to his feet. Mr. Turley was waiting.

"I was wondering what you were going to decide," the man said. "I think you chose best."

Deb nodded. His knees buckled and he sank to the ground. He opened his hand to stare at the silver piece.

"Here," Mr. Turley said. "Let me help you. . . . Why, you've got another one."

Deb looked up with a blank expression on his face.

"That penny," Mr. Turley said. "You've got another one." He reached into his pocket. "I was bringing—" He felt in his other pocket. "Well, I . . ."

Deb held the coin up. "It's here. It's the same. See my grandpa's marks on the back?"

"What? Now, how could that be?" Mr. Turley sank to his knees. "Never mind," he said. "I know how."

The two knelt together on the path beneath the leaden sky. The only sound was the drizzle of rain through the trees. At last Deb broke the silence. "Tell me, what is it? Where did it come from?"

Mr. Turley shivered and shook the rain out of his face. "Not here, it's too wet. We should get inside and get dry. You need food. And rest. Come. Let me help you up. Let's get in."

Chapter Twenty-eight

MR. TURLEY WAS QUIET as he ladled a bowl of stew for Deb. The food steamed in the cool air, and the smell of it was a welcome pleasure that made Deb's stomach growl. Mr. Turley broke off a chunk of bread from a round loaf and placed the meal on the table.

Deb sat in his nightshirt with a blanket wrapped about his shoulders. Once again, his borrowed clothes were hanging on a line before the hearth to dry.

"Have you ever seen a cherub cry?" Mr. Turley asked.

With a questioning look, Deb wiped the dribble of gravy from his chin.

"Or a fairy—an angel. An elf. Whichever you will." Mr. Turley held the penny up. Even in the dim light of the cabin it shone almost white. "There's a virtue in his tears."

He sat across from Deb and placed the coin on the table. "Eat up," he said. "There's plenty more." He dished his own bowl full.

They ate together in silence.

That night Deb lay snug and warm in the bed. The rain had stopped, and even inside the cabin the air felt clear and refreshed. Mr. Turley snored from beneath his blankets on the floor. He had insisted that Deb take the bed.

As Deb lay there, he fancied he could see a silver reflection on the ceiling, but that couldn't be—the night was dark and the penny still sat on the table where he had left it. He closed his eyes, and the reflection remained, painted on the back of his eyelids, so he knew it was only imagining—his fancy and Mr. Turley's story about the penny and a poor woman's hope.

She was young but already tired beyond her years. A long day of broken chances had worn her out and left her with little prospect. But at least the baby, slung across her chest in a shawl, had left off fussing. The daytime press on the streets had dwindled with the coming of evening. The crowds thinned, and the traffic gave over to just an occasional freight wagon. The woman hurried toward her lodgings, trying to beat nightfall, for after dark the streets of this quarter were perilous. As she passed the apothecary's corner, a boy begging alms thrust out his dirty hand. His red hair seemed out of place in this gray and dingy city.

"I have none," the woman said in a thin voice. She ducked her head and hurried by. But then she stopped and turned. "I've food," she said. "I can spare a bit of that. My home is close."

The boy nodded. "Thank'ee," he said.

It was a short way across the cobblestones and down an alley to a rickety flight of stairs. The woman led the way, the baby clutched tight. With the boy at her heels, she climbed past the first three landings.

"Be careful here." She nodded at the broken step and a long fall to the alleyway below. The boy took her outstretched hand and she guided him past the missing stair.

At the fourth landing, they came to a door. The young woman pushed against it with her shoulder. It squealed open to a dark apartment. The baby began to fuss again—a fitful whimpering that sounded for all the world like hunger.

"Shush, shush, my wee one." The mother rocked the baby in her arms. It calmed at her voice, and she laid it on the only piece of furniture in the room, a sagging bed with a threadbare covering. Then from a shelf on the wall she took a small bundle. "Here is some bread. It's not very much, but it's a great deal better than— Why, what's wrong?"

The boy had not moved from his spot just inside the door. He stood there still, his gaze turned to the floor. "I'm sorry," he said. He wiped his eyes with his hand. "I didn't know you was so wanting." He reached into his pocket. "Here, take this."

The woman's face brightened for an instant, but then she sank to the bed and shook her head.

"Please take it," he repeated. "I begged it from a royal gentleman in a golden carriage. 'Twas all he could spare, he said. And him being like a king. But you've a greater need."

"Oh, no. I couldn't. I've no right."

"But you have."

"No. I'm no beggar—" The woman stumbled to a halt. "Oh . . . I didn't mean to say—"

"It's only a loan, then."

She shook her head once more. "I couldn't repay you."

"Then just keep it till you can."

"But—"

"I'll come back for it one day. It *will* do you good."

He crossed the shabby room and took the woman's hand. And as he placed the small coin there, a single teardrop fell from his cheek and splashed upon the penny and her palm.

Deb rolled to his side. Sleep was coming. He could feel it seeping into his thoughts and through his legs and arms and hands. Mr. Turley's story was like a lullaby, filling him with a pleasant warmth. Earlier, he had asked where Mr. Turley learned the story. "The wee baby was my ma," he answered with a catch in his throat. "The woman was my grandmamma."

Deb thought of the beggar. Then he thought of the redheaded boy—Bray Skoolle, was that his name?—crouched alone, imprisoned in a circle of emptiness.

Chapter Twenty-nine

I CAN'T LEAVE him there," Deb said.

Mr. Turley put another log on the fire to help ward off the morning chill. "It's dangerous business."

"I know, but I've got to try."

Mr. Turley shook his head. "At least let me set you on your way."

"Yes, please. I'm afraid I'd just get lost again if you didn't." Deb wrapped up the bread Mr. Turley had given him and stuffed it in his bag. "You've been more than kind, like you were to my grandpa."

"He was a fine boy," Mr. Turley said.

Deb laughed. "He's not a boy anymore. He's an old man. Older than the trees."

"Don't matter. I'll always think of him as that boy

who was going to save my life, if he could. Now, how about some breakfast before I send you on your way?"

The day was bright by the time Mr. Turley led Deb up out of his valley. Only a few shreds of cloud hung on the horizon to remind them of the spent storm.

"Don't get caught again," Mr. Turley said. "Old Scratch has drawn too many circles in the dirt, trapped too many souls."

"I'll be careful. I've got the penny. I'll keep it close." Deb adjusted the bag over his shoulder. "I guess I'm ready."

"Then just follow this road to tomorrow. It should take you where you want to go."

Deb yearned to ask Mr. Turley to accompany him, to bring his comfort and security along the road between here and Deb's task. Instead, without another word, Deb turned and set out on his own, not wanting to be a cost to anyone else.

"Good luck," Mr. Turley called after him.

When night fell, Deb curled up in his blanket with the silver penny clutched in his hand. He couldn't sleep but felt he had to try. He feared what lay ahead. He feared the darkness about him. He feared that Old Scratch would appear out of nowhere to trap him again. He tried to think of other things, though it was difficult with the quiet night all about. He wondered if Ma missed him. He wondered if Tam still chattered on and on about things. He hoped so. He wondered if Grandpa still thought old stories were best. He hoped that, too.

He only slept when his eyes finally drooped shut on their own.

The next morning found him once again in familiar surroundings. He passed the field where Betsy had grazed. She was nowhere to be found. He thought to try calling, to see if she would come. He hesitated but then continued on his way.

Soon he was in sight of the poplars before the empty house. He slowed, still with no idea of what he could do to help Bray. By the time he reached the orchard, he was having second thoughts altogether. The hex of the circle was sure. He had felt its power. There didn't seem to be any way out.

He weaved his way through the orchard but stopped at the very edge of the trees. He ducked back behind a twisted trunk. Bray was not alone. The old man had returned.

"Looky here what I've got now!" the man cackled. He hopped from foot to foot. "My biggest prize!" He spun about and danced around the circle, more excited than when he'd caught Deb. "My own, my own, my own."

Deb shrank back behind the tree trunk. Now his task seemed impossible.

The old man pushed at Bray with a long finger. Bray didn't move. The man flashed his hand before Bray's face. He mussed the boy's red hair. He clapped his hands near his ears. Then he capered to the edge of the clearing and snapped a branch from a tree. With its sharp end he poked at the boy—at his back, his face. Still Bray did not flinch.

The old man wasn't content to have Bray's freedom. It seemed he wanted to hurt him, too.

Deb couldn't watch any longer. He had to do something. But what? What other hexes did this old man know? What other power did he hold?

The old man jabbed at Bray again and again. The look on his face had changed to one of cruel pleasure. His eyes turned wild and bright.

Deb could hardly breathe. With Grandpa's silver penny held outstretched before him, he stormed into the clearing. "Get away!" he cried. "Leave him be."

The old man spun about. He started forward with the branch raised, then recognized the talisman in Deb's hand. He dropped the stick and stepped back against the circle, spreading his arms as if to protect it from Deb's approach. He snarled.

"I'll have you both," he said. But there was uncertainty in his voice.

Deb continued forward. Strength flowed from the penny. "Get away."

The old man's eyes darted about. "He's mine, you—you can't have him. Go away."

"No. *You* go away." Deb held the penny up. It sparkled in the sunlight, casting a reflection that flitted about the clearing like it had a life of its own. The reflection touched the trees, the earth, Bray in his circle. It touched the old man on the forehead and he screamed—a cry that came from a place as deep as time.

He clasped his hands to his head and ran, sobbing, into the orchard. "Mine," he cried as he fled. "Mine. . . ."

Deb had been holding his breath. His knees gave out, and he stumbled to the earth. When his heart had settled a bit, he pulled himself to his feet and hurried to Bray's side.

"I'm here to help you," he said, "to get you out of there."

Bray didn't look up. He sat hunched in a ball, his face hidden in his arms. It was as if his spirit had flown to some other place. Deb reached out a hand and shook him. There was no response. Not a movement. Not a sound.

Deb pushed. Bray tumbled over against the invisible bounds of his prison, but no farther.

What had Bray said? *There must be a replacement?*

Deb could do what Bray had done—step into the circle and push. But then *he* would be trapped. He would be pulled into that oblivion in which Bray was lost. Deb remembered the thoughts he'd had as he hung from the cliff near Mr. Turley's cabin. He had almost let go then. At least now there was a benefit to be gained. Bray would be rescued.

He sat down on the ground to ponder his choice. He stared at the silver penny in his hand—the penny that had been touched by the other boy's tears. He thought of Tam and Grandpa and Ma and Pa. He remembered Grandpa's story and how he escaped the massacre through trickery and luck. He remembered the hopeful feeling the coin had given him when he lay helpless in bed, as if it did indeed have a life and will of its own. Then Deb had an idea, like it sprang up from the coin itself—the coin with the face of the old king. Would *it* count as a replacement? Would its magic be enough? He placed the penny inside the circle with King George the Second's head turned upward.

"Please work," he whispered.

He pushed at Bray once more. Bray rolled out of his prison to sprawl, facedown, in the orchard grass—in the spot where there should have been ashes from Grandpa's burnings. But this place wasn't the same. Deb would have to accept that.

Bray rolled over and sat up, blinking his eyes. "You came back," he said.

Deb nodded. "But I'm afraid I've lost your penny."

Chapter Thirty

LOOKY THERE," Bray said pointing to the sky. "A hawk. That's good luck."

The bird spiraled on invisible currents, a dark silhouette against the deep blue.

Deb examined the scratches on his arm. "Good luck? Maybe for some."

Bray nodded. "Good luck, for sure. Well, we best be on our way."

"Where to?" Deb asked.

Bray stared into his face. "Where do you want to go?"

Deb figured that what he wanted and what was likely were at complete odds. "To see Grandpa and Tam," Deb said. "And Ma and Pa and Lydia. But I'll go where you think I should."

"Do you know what's waiting for you back home? Your real home?"

Deb frowned in bewilderment. But then he remembered: a bed and a crutch and a twisted leg. He nodded.

"Is that what you want?"

There was only one answer. "Yes."

"Then follow me," Bray said.

The path they traveled clung to the stream as it wound its way toward the mountains that sprang out of the mists before them. The rolling hills grew into foothills. The stream leapt over rocks and splashed noisily into green pools. At the foot of a cascading waterfall Bray stopped. Deb divvied up Mr. Turley's bread.

"That's all there is," he said.

"'Twill suffice," Bray answered. "We'll not be needing more."

"Where are we going?" Deb asked. "Will there be food there?"

Bray nodded. "Food a-plenty. Some of the best cooking I've ever ate. But then that always comes with kindness. The surest hex there is."

Once they finished the bread they crossed through the stream and climbed up along the side of the rapids.

"Have a care," Bray called back to Deb.

But Deb didn't need the warning. The rocks were

slippery with mist, and the effort took all his attention. When he reached the top of the falls, Bray helped him over the last little bit.

Together they continued upward. They climbed through a canyon that wound deeper into the mountains. The creek had lost all pretense of peace. It rushed and roared from ledge to ledge. Deb gave up trying to keep dry. He struggled after Bray, who seemed undaunted by the effort of their climb.

At last they came upon another waterfall—a fall that plunged down a sheer cliff face, hiding the rocks beneath in a veil of white. Here they had to abandon the stream altogether. They found a trail that angled across a scree-covered slope. With bare feet Deb picked his way over the loose rock.

The hours stretched on, and the day closed about them. They passed the night huddled beneath a clump of scrub oak. Deb's legs ached, and he slept only little.

Through burning eyes he watched the sun rise and was taken aback at how high they had already climbed. Far below them the plains were a hazy tapestry of golden brown, dressed up with forest greens and blues.

"Let's go on," Bray said.

Deb groaned but hefted himself up and followed. For him the journey became a matter of setting one foot before the other. His knees hurt, and his thighs burned with the effort. When he felt he couldn't move another step, Bray would stop, unbidden, and allow Deb to catch his breath and steady the shaking in his legs. But then Bray would urge him on again and lead the way higher up the bare side of the mountain.

Every step became an effort, but somehow Deb pushed on, forgetting everything except the climb. Even the purpose of this journey became a vague wish that floated away.

The day passed, and the mountain turned rougher. Together, time and effort wore down Deb's resolve until he was sure that each next step would be his last. But still, with Bray leading the way, he continued.

"We're there," Bray said at last. "We're at the top."

Deb pulled himself up over the last ledge and stood with his eyes closed. The setting sun burned red through his lids. He felt cold and achy. His legs were leaden and his breath came deep and shuddering as if he couldn't get enough air.

"I need to rest," he said. He slumped down with his back to a giant boulder and pulled his knees up to his chest. "Wait for me."

But there was no answer.

He looked about. Bray was nowhere to be seen—not back down the steep slope they had just climbed nor here among the rocks. Deb bowed his head to his knees and, sitting there atop the world, too tired to care, he fell asleep.

It was a dream of music that woke him. But perhaps it was not a dream at all, for when Deb roused from his sleep the music continued—a melody that settled directly into his heart. He opened his eyes. Bray sat cross-legged before him, singing words Deb couldn't understand. Bray clutched a small bundle of sticks and as he sang he pulled twigs from his hand and set them on the ground before him. Deb watched in fascination, though whether entranced by the boy's actions or the music he couldn't tell.

At last Bray stopped his singing—though the sound of it seemed to continue somewhere inside of Deb. Without looking up Bray said, "Let's go."

Deb didn't want to move. "I . . . I'm tired," he said. "I need to rest before I climb down."

"Come," Bray insisted, rising to his feet.

Still not willing to disturb the echoes of music, Deb hesitated.

"It's just a short way," the boy said and held out his hand.

At last Deb allowed Bray to pull him up. Reluctantly he turned to the west. But his breath caught in his throat and his knees near buckled out from beneath him. He reached back with his hand. "What is it?"

Bray pushed from behind.

Before Deb could catch himself he stumbled forward into a blinding mist. The ground gave out beneath him and he slid down an invisible slope. But then that, too, gave way. As he fell the mist grew so thick he could almost feel it. At first it had been gray and damp. Now it turned dark and hard. Though he kicked and struggled and fought against it, it swallowed him whole. He pushed at it and felt a thousand needle pricks in his hands and fingers. And then he thought he heard a sound. He strained to catch it—a faint *tick-tick*, like the scratching of mice behind a wall. A glimmer of light flashed before his eyes and faded away, leaving behind a jagged pattern. He focused on the sound, trying to trace it as it spun round in his head. He clinched his eyes closed, then opened them wide.

The sound became familiar, and bright daylight flooded his mind.

"Grandpa," he heard a voice say. "Look, he's here. He's back."

"So he is," another voice replied. "So he is."

Chapter Thirty-one

*T*AM SAT at the foot of Aunt Mary's bed and fought back both tears and laughter. Her insides were all confused with not knowing how to act—she felt like crying and singing and shouting all at once. Instead she just twisted her apron in her hands while Deb leaned against the headboard and sipped the broth that Aunt Mary spooned from a bowl.

"Do you want any more?" Aunt Mary asked.

"No," Deb said, his voice still light with weakness. "That's enough for now." Then he looked at Tam with eyes brighter than she could ever remember. "I'm sorry I was cross with you before."

"Oh, no," Tam said, hurrying to his side. "*I'm* sorry. I didn't under—"

"It's all right." Deb squeezed her hand. "It's going to be all right. I'll be just fine." He stretched his arms out before him. "See, they're healed. The scratches are gone." He let them drop to the quilt.

Tam wanted to ask what he meant, but Deb continued speaking. "Would you fetch me my crutch?"

"Dear," Aunt Mary said, "you know you can't get up just yet."

"I know. I just want to see my crutch. I guess we need to get acquainted."

Tam wondered if Deb was still a mite funny in the head, but she ran upstairs and retrieved the crutch anyway. When she returned, she laid it across her cousin's lap. He ran a hand over its polished surface.

"Look," he said. "My name's even on it."

"Bray put it there," she said.

"Is he anywhere about?"

"No," Aunt Mary answered. "We haven't seen him since the night after you fell."

"I think he's gone away," Tam said.

Deb held a silver coin up in his other hand. He looked at it in amazement, as if wondering how it came to be there. "Not yet he hasn't," he said. "Not without this."

Tam stood back and looked at her cousin. The very last of the premonitions slipped away, and peace settled in her heart.

"I've missed you," she whispered.

Though her words were light as air, barely audible, still Deb nodded in return. "Thanks for helping me back."

"But I never did anything."

"It's the thought that counts."

Chapter Thirty-two

LATER THAT AFTERNOON, Grandpa sat alone by the creek, under the overhanging boughs of an apple tree. He looked up into the branches and sighed. In his hand he held the silver penny that Deb had given back just that morning. Deb had said he didn't need its luck anymore. Grandpa shook his head at the recollection.

"Everyone needs luck," he said to his trees.

"Not everyone," someone answered.

Bray Skoolle stood on the far side of the creek, his hair coppery bright in the sunlight.

Grandpa held up the penny. "I lost my pa and brothers—and my own son—because its luck wasn't near enough for us all."

"Mayhaps they was fated otherwise."

Grandpa scowled. "Fate? Then she's a cruel one."

Bray laughed out loud. "Fate or luck. They're two sides to the same coin."

"But what about my great-grandson? He needs a bit of luck yet. His leg—"

"Maybe he has his own luck."

Grandpa shook his head.

"He does."

"Well, I don't know . . ."

"He does. And now if you don't mind, I would like—"

But Grandpa didn't want to hear the request. He was afraid he knew what it was going to be, and he wasn't ready to let the coin go. "I've a question myself," he said. "Old King George has been with me for ever so long. Why did—"

It was Bray's turn to interrupt. "Why'd it go to Deb? Maybe because *you* don't need the luck anymore."

Grandpa couldn't help but smile at hearing his great-grandson's words again. "Maybe so."

He thought for a moment, his gaze fixed on the penny that lay on his palm. "Maybe so," he repeated. And then, with a flick of his wrist, he tossed the coin across the tumbling water. It flashed once in the sunlight and disappeared into Bray's outstretched hand.

"Thank'ee, Alvin Corey," the boy said. He shoved the penny into the pocket of his ragged overalls and turned to walk up the far path, disappearing around a thistle-grown bend.

Grandpa shook his head. "I hope he don't mind those marks I put on the coin. I surely hope he don't mind."

And the answer came to him, as clear as if spoken aloud. "He don't mind at all."

About the Author

RANDALL WRIGHT lives in Utah with his wife and children. He longs for a silver penny of his own, but understands that luck often has its own designs. He is the author of two other novels for young readers, *Hunchback* and *A Hundred Days from Home*.